*Jenny stood back and
scrutinized her efforts.*

It was amazing the difference some increased color and a little extra mascara could make.

Her blue eyes looked bigger and more than a little mysterious.

The darker lipstick enhanced the natural fullness of her lips.

Pleased with the results, she grabbed the bottle of perfume Marcee had given her for her birthday. The sultry scent couldn't have been more of a contrast to her normal Lily-of-the-Valley fragrance.

After she'd hit all the pulse points—and a few more places for good measure—she faced the mirror.

This time a stranger stared back.

A woman confident in her sexuality.

A woman who embraced life instead of sitting on the sidelines.

A woman capable of doing something wild and just a little bit crazy . . .

When She Was Bad

CINDY KIRK

AVON BOOKS
An Imprint of HarperCollinsPublishers

This is a work of fiction. Names, characters, places, and incidents are products of the author's imagination or are used fictitiously and are not to be construed as real. Any resemblance to actual events, locales, organizations, or persons, living or dead, is entirely coincidental.

AVON BOOKS
An Imprint of HarperCollins*Publishers*
10 East 53rd Street
New York, New York 10022-5299

Copyright © 2007 by Cindy Kirk
ISBN: 978-0-06-084790-6
ISBN-10: 0-06-084790-5
www.avonromance.com

First Avon Books paperback printing: July 2007

Avon Trademark Reg. U.S. Pat. Off. and in Other Countries, Marca Registrada, Hecho en U.S.A.
HarperCollins® is a registered trademark of HarperCollins Publishers.

Printed in the U.S.A.

10 9 8 7 6 5 4 3 2 1

Acknowledgments

Thanks to Nancy Chase, Accountant Extra-ordinaire. Any accurate portrayals of life in the accounting world must be attributed to her. Any mistakes are my own.

One

"Want to get laid tonight?"

Jennifer Carman didn't need to look up from her computer to know who was standing in her office doorway. Only one person would announce herself in such a manner.

Jenny hit save, swiveled her chair, and smiled at the flamboyant redhead. "Let me check my calendar."

She shot a cursory glance at the planner sitting open on her desk and shook her head. "Sorry. Getting laid isn't on my schedule. And if it's not on my schedule—"

"I know." Marcee Robbens heaved a dramatic sigh. "It's not going to happen."

Dressed in a tailored navy suit, crisp white blouse, and closed-toe shoes, Marcee looked every inch a corporate executive. But the devilish sparkle in her green eyes and the short skirt revealing a pair of fabulous legs said there was more to this CPA than a tax table and calculator.

Jenny lifted a brow. "I thought you'd be on the train and halfway to suburbia by now."

Marcee laughed as if Jenny had said something ridiculously funny. "It's Friday night. The last place I want to be is home."

Jenny smiled ruefully. Marcee embraced the Chicago nightlife with a passion and always had something planned for the weekends. Jenny was usually so engrossed in work, she barely noticed when Friday rolled around.

"A bunch of us are going to grab some dinner, then hit the clubs." Marcee took a seat in the leather wingback in front of Jenny's desk and crossed one long leg over the other. "Why don't you come? Clint from Legal will be there. He thinks you're a real hottie."

"Clint Daniels?" Jenny furrowed her brow. "The thin guy with the hair that always looks like it needs a trim?"

"Who cares about his hair?" Marcee's cinnamon-colored lips turned upward. "The guy has a really nice ass."

"Clint does have a nice, uh, backside," Jenny said. "But we can't be talking about the same person."

"There's only one Clint," Marcee said with a wink.

The man Jenny was thinking of had started with the firm last year and was kind of cute, if you liked that starving poet look. But the last time she'd talked to him, he had a ring on his finger. "The Clint I'm thinking of is married."

Marcee rolled her eyes. "You are so out of touch. He and his wife split last month."

Jenny frowned. "And he's already going out?"

"What's he supposed to do?" Genuine surprise skittered across Marcee's face. "Sit home and cry?"

"I can't believe he's put himself back on the dating block so soon." Marriage was sacred to Jenny. If she was in Clint's position, sitting home and crying was just what she'd be doing.

Marcee ignored the comment and tilted her head. "So, will you come?"

"I'd like to, but tonight isn't good." Jenny made a conscious effort to inject a note of true regret in her tone. After all, she *did* appreciate the invitation. "I already have plans."

Marcee straightened in the chair, her eyes bright with interest. "A date?"

For a second, Jenny was tempted to say yes. Maybe come up with some far-fetched tale about a visiting prince and a stretch limousine. Or a sexy construction worker and a rugged 4x4. When she was a teenager, Jenny had loved to make up stories.

"Tell me about him," Marcee urged, apparently taking Jenny's silence for assent. "Is he hot?"

Jenny opened her mouth, then shut it, reminding herself she was an adult and lying wasn't a good thing. Even if it did make a dull life more interesting.

"No date." Jenny shook her head. "I'm helping my family clean my grandmother's house tomorrow, and I need to get to bed early."

"Cleaning?" Marcie wrinkled her nose.

"I don't really have a choice." Jenny sighed. None of them did. They'd put off the sad task as long as possible. Sorting through Gram's personal items and readying her house for sale had to be done. If only it didn't make her death seem so, well, final.

Jenny's heart clenched, and she brushed away sudden tears.

Marcee's expression softened in sympathy. "Is this your grandma who died in that car accident a couple of months ago?"

Jenny nodded. Gram had been a young seventy-five, active in her church and in the community. She'd been a good driver, too. But that hadn't mattered. A speeding car had rear-ended her tiny import while she was sitting at a traffic light.

"She'd have wanted you to go out with your friends and have a good time," Marcee said in a persuasive tone. "You know she would."

Marcee, the silver-tongued temptress. The thought brought the smile back to Jenny's lips. Her friend had a way of making even the most irresponsible actions seem rational.

But this time Jenny wasn't going to cave. She'd been out with Marcee and her friends, and she knew the drill. Things didn't get going until at least ten, sometimes eleven. Jenny hoped to be fast asleep by then.

Besides, the last time she'd gone out had been painful. Marcee had urged her to ask a cute guy to dance. When she'd finally gathered up her courage, her tongue had stumbled over the words. He'd stared at her as if she were from another planet. Her stomach knotted, just remembering.

"I still have a lot of work to do." Jenny gestured a hand toward her computer screen. "Once I leave here I'm going straight to bed."

"Going to bed beats sitting in a bar any day," Marcee said with an impish smile. "I just hope you're not sleeping alone."

Marcee wiggled her brows, and Jenny laughed.

"Is sex all you ever think about?"

Her friend's smile widened. "What else is there when you're young and single?"

There'd been a time when Jenny would have been horrified by such a comment. But now Marcee's irreverence was one of the things Jenny liked most about her. Marcee's freewheeling lifestyle might be totally at odds with Jenny's upbringing, but she was fun.

"Sure you won't change your mind?" Marcee pulled a compact out of her purse and peered at Jenny over the top of the mirror. "You always have a good time when we go out."

Jenny rolled her eyes. Marcee made it sound like she was a regular party animal. Technically she'd gone out with Marcee only twice, and each time she'd headed home after one drink. But Marcee was right, she enjoyed socializing with her single coworkers.

All Jenny's other friends were married with families. It had been fun to be around people who talked about something other than babies and husbands.

"I'm sure I'd have a blast," Jenny said. "But tonight just isn't going to work."

"You don't have to get laid," Marcee said. "Unless you happen to run across some really hot guy and—"

"Marcee." Jenny raised one hand. She could tell where this was headed, and it was a place she didn't want to go.

Talking about sex made her uncomfortable. Even when Jenny had been in a relationship, she'd considered what she did—or didn't do—behind closed doors to be her own business.

"But—"

"I can't go tonight," Jenny said. "Not for a drink. Or to get laid. I have to finish this audit."

Marcee stared at Jenny for a long moment. "I'll let you off the hook this time. But you, my dear, really need to get out and live a little. If you don't, you're going to wake up one day and realize you gave the best years of your life to a company that didn't give a shit about you."

By the time Marcee finished speaking, her voice was loud and strident. Jenny had to smile. The only other thing she'd seen Marcee so passionate about was sex. "Tell me how you really feel."

"Smile all you want." Marcee stood and adjusted her short skirt. "But I've worked here a long time, and I've seen it happen over and over. This company eats up dedicated people and spits them out. Trust me; working these long hours isn't worth it."

"It will be if it gets me that promotion," Jenny said. "Rich told me today that he plans to name another manager before the end of the month."

Rich Dodson and his brother, Chuck, ran the prestigious CPA firm founded by their father over forty years ago. On more than one occasion Rich had told Jenny how impressed he was with how she dealt with her clients. In a roundabout way he'd implied the next step up the ladder was hers for the taking.

Concern filled Marcee's eyes. "You deserve to be a manager, no doubt about it. But that doesn't always mean anything. Not in this company."

"I'll get it." Jenny shoved aside a twinge of uncertainty. "Haven't you heard that good things come to those who wait? And I've been waiting a long time for this."

The shoebox in Jenny's lap overflowed with black and white photographs from a bygone era. The photo albums Jenny had already retrieved from her grandmother's closet had been filled with pictures of family, but these loose photos all appeared to be of Gram and her friend Jasmine Coret.

Jenny told herself she didn't have time to look. Still, her gaze lowered, and Jasmine Coret smiled back at her.

Though Jenny had never met the woman, she recognized her instantly. Jasmine had been her grandmother's best friend when she'd been young, and a picture of her had sat atop Gram's piano for as long as Jenny could remember. She'd died when she was Jenny's age, but Gram had frequently said Jasmine packed more living into her thirty years than most people did in a lifetime.

Jenny held a colorized photograph up to the light. The stylish hat on the woman's auburn curls sat at a saucy angle, and she'd puckered her red-painted lips for the camera, as if blowing a kiss to the photographer. She looked so happy and carefree that Jenny couldn't help but smile back.

In the next photo, a handsome soldier in uniform gazed at Jasmine as if she were the only woman in the world. Jenny's heart twisted. What would it be like to spark such adoration?

It didn't seem fair. Jasmine's life had been filled with fun, excitement, and handsome men. Jenny's life was filled with spreadsheets, long hours, and men who never gave her a second look.

"Get back to work," Jenny's teenage sister called out from across the room

Jenny stared at the picture for a moment longer before returning it to the box. Annie was right. There was no time for a pity party. Not when there was work to do.

She'd just taken the last dress from her grandmother's bedroom closet when she discovered another box at the back of the top shelf. Standing on her tiptoes, Jenny lifted it down carefully, wondering what she'd find this time. She'd already found a number of items Gram had squirreled away; a gift set of towels still in the cellophane in the back of the linen closet and a pair of brand-new crystal earrings in a jewelry chest.

Jenny placed the box on the bed and lifted the lid, anticipation fueling her movements. But the moment her gaze settled on the decorative vase surrounded by shiny foil, a wave of sadness washed over her, and she wished she'd left it on the shelf.

"It's still in the wrapping paper," she said, almost to herself.

Annie, curious as a cat, scrambled to her feet and peered over her shoulder. "Isn't that the vase you got Gram?"

"Five years ago." Jenny caressed the deep red glass with a fingertip. "I bought it out of my first paycheck from Dodson and Dodson."

Her grandmother had seen the antique cranberry vase in a store in Long Grove and had instantly fallen in love with it. Unbeknownst to her grandmother, Jenny had gone back and bought it for her birthday.

Jenny lifted a puzzled gaze. "She never used it."

Though she'd tried to speak matter-of-factly, Jenny couldn't keep the disappointment from her voice. She thought she'd given her grandmother something she liked . . .

"Are you almost finished?" Jenny's mother bustled into the room and lowered an armful of bedding into a large cardboard box on the floor. In her mid-fifties, she looked like an older version of her two daughters. Although her hair had darkened from the honey blond of her youth, her eyes were the same bright blue, and her laugh just as infectious.

Life had been good to Carol Carman, and it showed. She straightened, and a questioning look crossed her face. "Jennifer?"

"Gram didn't like Jenny's gift," Annie announced.

"I thought she did." Jenny tried to smile, but her lips refused to cooperate. "I guess I was wrong."

"I'm not sure I know the gift you're talking about." Carol stepped over the pile of shoes Annie had been sorting and moved to the bed. "What was it?"

"A vase." Jenny lifted the box for her mother's inspection.

The minute her mother's eyes lit on the cranberry-colored glass, her lips curved up in a smile. "I remember this. You gave it to her the year we had her birthday celebration at Maggiano's. She was so happy she cried."

"So happy she took it home and shoved it in the back of the closet," Annie said with customary bluntness. "That's what I do with gifts I *don't* like."

To Jenny's surprise her mother laughed.

"That's what I do, too," Carol said. "But my mother wasn't like us. She was more like Jenny. She put things she treasured away for safekeeping, waiting for just the right time to use them."

"I don't do that," Jenny protested.

Carol and Annie exchanged a knowing smile, and Jenny could feel her face warm.

"I use what I'm given," Jenny insisted.

"What about those placemats and napkin rings I got you for Christmas?" her mother asked. "I haven't seen those on your table. Didn't you like them?"

"I love them," Jenny said. "I just haven't had any company and—"

"See. You're just like Gram," Annie said with a superior smile. "Isn't she, Mom?"

But her mother was too smart to be so easily drawn into choosing sides. Carol's face softened. "All I'm saying is Gram loved your gift. Don't think she didn't."

Jenny shoved the foil around the vase and replaced the lid on the box. She was too tired to argue. What did it matter now anyway? She held the box out to her mother.

Carol shook her head. "Gram would have wanted you to have it."

Jenny sighed. She supposed she'd keep the vase. Though it was too formal for her apartment, she'd find a place for it. And every time she looked at it, she'd remember all the times she and Gram spent "antiquing" together in Long Grove.

Happy times they'd never again share. A tightness gripped her heart, and Jenny found herself blinking back tears. "I miss her so much."

Annie lowered her gaze, her normally animated face uncharacteristically solemn. "She won't be there to see me graduate next year."

"She always joked that she'd dance all night at my wedding." The lump in Jenny's throat grew thicker as memories flooded back.

"She had a good life." Her mother cleared her throat, and her eyes shimmered with tears. She awkwardly patted Jenny's shoulder. "Her car accident should be a reminder to all of us. We need to enjoy the here and now because we never know when God will call us home."

"*Carpe diem.*" Annie nodded. "That's my motto."

Jenny knew she shouldn't laugh but she couldn't help it. Annie had never been particularly introspective, and if the stylish teenager wanted a motto, "I'll shop till I drop," would probably be more appropriate. "Do you even know what *carpe diem means*?"

Annie's eyes flashed. "You think you're the only smart one in this family?"

Her mother shot Jenny a you'd-better-take-care-of-this-right-now look.

"I never said you weren't smart," Jenny said quickly. Annie might have blond hair, but they all knew she had a redhead's temper.

Unfortunately, the look on Annie's face said she wasn't about to be easily appeased.

"Valedictorian," Annie spat the word. "Straight A's. Big deal. At least I haven't spent my high school years sitting home on the weekends. At least boys like me."

"Boys like me." The childish words were out of Jenny's mouth before she could stop them.

"Girls." Carol's eyes flashed a warning. "I know we're all a bit on edge, but let's try and be nice."

"I know what *carpe diem* means," Annie said, apparently determined to get the last word. "And I'm never going to let life pass *me* by."

"I don't think there's any danger of that."

Carol chuckled. "You seize every moment and then some."

The irritation on Annie's face eased at her mother's obvious approval.

"I do my best." Annie shot Jenny a smug look. She tossed her head, sending her long hair cascading down her back.

"I know you do," her mother said.

What about me? Jenny wanted to ask. *Don't you think I'm doing my best?* But Jenny stayed silent. She already had a good idea what her mother would say. When she'd turned thirty last year, her parents had made it very clear that they thought she was putting way too much emphasis on her career. That there was more to life than professional success.

Which was all well and good, if she had a personal life clamoring for attention. But she didn't. Other than Marcee, her friends were all married, most with kids. Her career was all she had, and she was proud of what she'd accomplished.

She might not be good socially, but she was a dynamite accountant. That's why, when her engagement had ended, she'd decided to focus on her strengths.

The problem was that many of her parents' friends were already grandparents, and her mom and dad were getting itchy for the pitter-patter of little feet. Hence the push for a "balanced life."

Still, considering how supportive they'd been in the past, her parents' attitude hurt. Sure she was working long hours and her social life was teetering on the edge of nonexistent, but she was also on the verge of success.

Jenny's fingers tightened on the box in her hands. Why couldn't they see that she didn't have time to invest in a relationship now?

There would be plenty of time later for balance . . . once she got the promotion.

Two

Though it was after four when Jenny finished her meeting in Naperville, she headed back to the office, hoping to get in a few more hours of work.

She was so far behind she didn't know how she was going to catch up. And she had no one to blame but herself. Instead of working late, she'd spent every night this week at her grandmother's house helping her mother and sister. But now that sad task was completed, and she was ready to dig into the work on her desk.

Jenny had discovered long ago that Friday afternoons were a good time to get things done. Most of the staff left early and there were few distractions.

Once off the elevator, Jenny made a beeline for her office, automatically pulling the door shut behind her. The large desk chair beckoned and Jenny took a seat and leaned back, letting the stress of the day melt away. After a moment, ready to face the night, Jenny signed on to her computer.

Her heart skipped a beat at the company-wide announcement on the intranet. D&D's long-awaited promotions had been announced.

Excitement skittered up her spine and Jenny searched the list, but the only manager listed in the e-mail was one of her coworkers.

Steve Croft.

She stared at the name, unable to believe what she was reading.

Steve, who had less seniority. Steve, who often left early to golf. Steve, who laughingly joked that his day began at nine and ended at four.

She didn't necessarily dislike the guy, but what was her boss thinking? Steve wasn't overly smart or particularly good with the clients. He was an okay employee but not outstanding. He certainly didn't have her dedication or experience.

But he *was* one of Rich's drinking buddies. And apparently that had been enough.

Jenny pulled her hands into fists. All her hard work and sacrifice had been for nothing. Anger rose up to choke her. The four walls closed in, pulling the breath from her throat. She had to get out before she sent a scathing e-mail saying exactly how she felt about her boss and his choice of manager.

But where to go?

Did it even matter? Anywhere was preferable to this place.

She powered down her computer and reached for her briefcase. A knock sounded on her office door, and Jenny jumped to her feet.

The knob twisted but didn't open, and Jenny realized she must have inadvertently locked it behind her.

"You can lock me out but you cannot hide."

The instant Jenny heard Marcee's voice, she couldn't help but smile.

Something told her she was about to get an offer to do something wild and crazy.

And this time she was going to say yes.

"You look like an accountant." Marcee studied Jenny with an intensity usually reserved for the toughest accounting problems. "You'll never get a man to notice, much less sleep with you looking like that."

Jenny had spent the last hour railing against the injustice of Steve's promotion, and surprisingly, Marcee had been a sympathetic listener.

She'd also taken the high road. Jenny hadn't heard a single I-told-you-so from the redhead.

But now Marcee was ready to grab some dinner and hit the bars. And once again, Jenny realized she'd been found lacking. "I could go home . . ."

Marcee shook her head. "I'm not letting you change your mind this time. We'll figure something out."

Jenny glanced down at her oatmeal-colored suit and wrinkled her nose. Marcee was right. The skirt and jacket were too . . . well . . . conservative. Too much like the Jennifer Carman who went to church every Sunday. Too much like the Jennifer Carman who'd passed her CPA exam with a near-perfect score. Too much like the Jennifer Carman who'd been living for her job and hadn't had sex in six long years.

Though the last time hadn't been that great, the thought of being intimate with a man did some very strange things to her insides. She pressed her legs tightly together but the ache remained.

"What do you have on underneath?" Marcee asked abruptly. "You still wearing the sexy stuff?"

Jenny nodded. One Christmas, she and Marcee had gone shopping and Marcee had discovered Jenny's secret passion—racy underwear, the skimpier the better. Today, underneath the conservative suit she wore a lacy red camisole and matching thong panties.

"Let me see it," Marcee demanded.

"Why?"

"I've got an idea."

Jenny slowly unbuttoned her jacket, and Marcee's red-painted lips widened into a broad smile.

"Perfect," Marcee said. "The skirt and camisole look great together. Once we get you some decent shoes, you're in business."

Jenny glanced down at her serviceable pumps.

"I've got an extra pair of stilettos in my office closet. We wear the same size so they should work." Marcee rose from the chair and pulled a makeup bag out of her purse. "I'll go get them. In the meantime, see what you can do with your eyes and lips."

Jenny was on her feet before Marcee had pulled the door shut. She went to the wardrobe in the corner of the room and opened the door. A full-length mirror hung on the inside.

Slipping her jacket off, Jenny stood in front of the glass and tried to see herself through a man's eyes. The breasts she'd cursed as a young girl were large enough to capture a man's imagination. She'd loved it when her former boyfriend used to cup them in his hands and rub his thumbs across the tips. And when he'd cover one with his mouth, she'd wished the night would never end.

Unfortunately, Michael had never lingered long. From the beginning he'd been more of a get-on, get-off kind of guy.

At first Jenny had thought it was because this was new territory for both of them. But she'd read enough articles in magazines and seen enough movies to know making love could be so much more fulfilling.

She still remembered the day she'd decided to take it upon herself to spice up their sex life. She'd stocked some honey in her bedside table with the idea of tempting Michael's appetite in a new way. He'd looked at her as if she'd just asked him to murder the pope. Her face had heated to burning but she hadn't given up, sure he'd love it if he'd just give it a try.

But he wouldn't consider it. Even after all these years she still remembered his words. He'd told her what she was suggesting was *perverted*.

She'd been embarrassed, then angry. She wasn't suggesting bestiality or a ménage à trois, merely that he drizzle a little warm honey on a few strategic locations to make their love-making extra sweet.

Her lips tightened. According to Michael, a decent woman would never have *thought* of such a thing, much less *suggested* it. She hadn't made any more suggestions. Why would she? After all, if he'd found the honey idea decadent, what would he have thought if she'd brought up different positions or locations?

Jenny sighed and turned back to the mirror. She realized suddenly it was after that episode that she'd become less spontaneous, less of a risk taker.

Carpe diem.

Her mother had been right. She'd put off living for way too long.

Jenny studied her reflection. Marcee had been right, too. Her hair passed muster but her makeup . . .

Jenny's gaze narrowed. Neutral-colored eye shadow and coral lip gloss might be perfect for the office, but it didn't fit her current mood.

She grabbed the makeup bag Marcee had left, pulled out several eye shadow palettes and some blush, and went to work.

Ten minutes later she stood back and scrutinized her efforts. It was amazing the difference some increased color and a little extra mascara could make.

Her blue eyes looked bigger and more than a little mysterious. The darker lipstick enhanced the natural fullness of her lips.

Pleased with the results, Jenny opened the desk drawer and grabbed the bottle of perfume Marcee had given her for her birthday. The sultry scent couldn't have been more of a contrast to her normal lily-of-the-valley fragrance.

When she'd hit all her pulse points—and a few more places for good measure—Jenny faced the mirror. This time a stranger stared back.

A woman confident in her sexuality.

A woman who embraced life instead of sitting on the sidelines.

A woman capable of doing something wild and just a little bit crazy.

O'Malley's was packed. The Cubs were playing and fans were out in force. Televisions mounted strategically on the wood-paneled walls of the popular Lincoln Park sports bar guaranteed everyone a good view of the game.

Jenny paused in the doorway and inhaled the smoke, beer, and sweat. A shiver of excitement traveled up her spine. She'd been here before, but tonight felt different. Or maybe *she* was different, ready to finally let go of her inhibitions and seize the day.

Marcee pushed through the crowd, sure-footed despite her spiky heels. Jenny followed, letting her hips sway gently from side to side, hoping at least one or two men were checking her out . . .

The crack of a bat split the air, and Jenny shifted her gaze to the nearest television in time to see a Cubs player round third base.

When he slid into home plate, a tall man sitting at a nearby table let out a roar of approval and jumped to his feet, sending his chair tumbling backward.

Marcee shrieked as the chair caught her leg. Her arms flailed. She fought to regain her balance.

Jenny immediately reached out a steadying hand but she wasn't quick enough. The tall guy had already slipped an arm around Marcee and pulled her close, stopping her fall.

"Why don't you watch—"

Marcee's outrage lasted but a second. Just long enough to get a good look at the man who now held her. Though Marcee had often told Jenny she preferred men with dark hair, Jenny had the feeling an exception would be made for this sandy-haired hunk.

Marcee brushed away a strand of hair with the back of her hand. Her green eyes shone dark and mysterious in the bar's dim light.

"Wow." Pure masculine appreciation filled the man's gaze.

Jenny understood. Not only did her friend have a pretty face, but with the short pleated skirt showing off her legs and a form-fitting top accentuating her curves, sex appeal could have been Marcee's middle name.

"Sorry about the chair," he said with a sheepish smile. "I get a little wild somtimes."

Marcee tilted her head back and studied him through lowered lashes. "And what's wrong with that?"

"Nothing. Nothing at all," the man said hurriedly, his smile widening at her suggestive tone. "So am I forgiven?"

"You are," Marcee said. "As long as you buy me a drink."

"A drink?" The man chuckled. "Honey, I'll buy you all the drinks you can handle and then some."

Marcee's lips curved slowly upward and the guy pulled her closer.

Jenny sighed. Less than five minutes in the bar and she'd already been relegated to third-wheel status. She glanced longingly at the door.

Marcee caught the glance and her gaze narrowed. She untangled herself from the hunk's arms and gave him a gentle shove.

"I'll catch you at the bar," Marcee said. "I need to talk to my friend."

"Friend?" A momentary look of surprise crossed the man's face, and Jenny realized with a pang that despite her new look, she'd blended into the woodwork.

But when the man shifted his gaze, he didn't immediately dismiss her as she'd expected. Instead, his gaze lingered. "Well, hel-lo, beautiful."

It was nice, Jenny thought, for him to act interested. But totally unnecessary.

Marcee seemed to agree. Her eyes narrowed slightly, and she slid her hand up the man's arm to regain his attention.

"You can get me a Sam Adams." Marcee slanted a sideways glance at Jenny. "And my friend will have—?"

Jenny hadn't heard the man offer to buy *her* a drink but he seemed agreeable. "White wine, please."

"A Sam Adams and a white wine." Marcee repeated the order, flashed him a brilliant smile, and turned her attention back to Jenny.

The man hesitated for a second, then headed toward the bar.

"Don't you want to go with him?"

Jenny had seen how Marcee and the guy looked at each other. The last thing she wanted was to stand in the way of true lust. "Just say the word if you want me to leave—"

"If I want you to leave?" What looked like genuine surprise skittered across Marcee's face. "What kind of crazy talk is that?"

"I thought maybe you'd want to hook up." Surely Marcee didn't need her to spell it out. "You know. Three's a crowd and all that."

"Don't be silly. I'm not ready to hook up with anyone. Not yet anyway." Marcee slipped her arm through Jenny's. "This night is about *you*, not me."

It was also, Jenny feared, her last chance. If she didn't spread her wings now, something told her she might end up grounded for life.

"I want tonight to be different." With a start, Jenny realized how much she meant the words. "I'm just afraid it will end up being more of the same."

Marcee's gaze turned thoughtful. "Remember last year when you were assigned the Hanover account?"

How could Jenny forget? It had been the most complicated audit she'd ever coordinated. Merely remembering that time made her heart beat faster. "It was a career make-or-break situation."

"But you pulled it off." Admiration filled Marcee's voice. "You didn't let fear stop you."

Jenny had pulled it off because of Bev. A partner at D&D, Beverly Tompkins was an expert in the area of corporate auditing. Before Jenny had walked into Hanover Companies, she'd asked herself how Bev would approach the audit. She'd realized immediately that one of Bev's strengths was her confident demeanor. If she was unsure, it never showed. Jenny had been determined to exude that same level of confidence. The weird thing was, she'd quickly discovered that merely *acting* confident made her feel more confident.

Jenny thought for a moment. Playacting had helped her overcome her audit jitters. Maybe it could help tonight, too.

But who to emulate?

Marcee?

No way. Jenny loved Marcee dearly, but her friend was way too over-the-top.

Mary Sue?

Her cousin might be great at charity fund-raisers and church events, but if Marcee was over-the-top, Mary Sue was buried in the basement.

Jenny sighed and thought a little harder.

Jasmine?

The image of the vivacious woman in the photo danced before Jenny's eyes. Every instinct told her that Jasmine was perfect. Not only had her grandmother's friend been beautiful and flirtatious, she appeared to be the kind of woman who didn't have a care in the world. In her short life she'd perfected the art of living for today.

Jasmine wouldn't be *worrying* about having a good time tonight, she'd be making it happen.

Jenny took a deep breath.

"Tonight is going to work out." She felt herself gain strength with each word. "I know it."

Marcee nodded her approval. "Now you're talking."

"Why don't we get a table?" Jenny scanned the bar. "There's an empty one over by the pool tables. We'd have a good view of the room."

Now that she'd fully committed herself to an evening of excitement, Jenny was eager to get started.

"Good idea." Marcee pulled a compact from her tiny purse and checked her makeup. "Check out Mr. Tall Texan on your way there."

"What do you mean?" Jenny frowned. "Aren't you coming?"

"In a minute." Marcee snapped the compact closed. "I've got a few things to do first."

The redhead's gaze slid to a group of men standing off to the side talking.

Jenny just smiled and wove her way through the crowd, at the last minute remembering to check out the guy at the bar. She immediately knew the one who'd caught Marcee's eye; a tall, dark-haired man who looked like he'd ridden into town on a horse. While he was attractive, with chiseled features and a strong jaw, he didn't make Jenny's pulse quicken. And she'd never liked guys with mustaches.

A roar of laughter sounded from the pool tables. Jenny turned slightly to get a better look. Her gaze settled on a slender man with wire-rimmed glasses. He had the body of a runner, and his clothes were stylish but not flashy. She couldn't say he was handsome, but he was definitely above average. Instead of looking away, she boldly let her gaze linger.

He caught her staring and smiled. Putting down his pool cue, the man motioned her over.

Jenny forced herself to smile back, knowing Jasmine wouldn't let such an opportunity pass her by. Wiping her suddenly sweaty palms against her skirt, she started toward him.

About ten feet separated them when Jenny noticed his left hand. She stopped and looked again. It *was* a ring. Disappointment sluiced through her.

He called to her when she turned around but Jenny ignored him.

No matter how much she liked his open, friendly smile, the thin gold band encircling his ring finger made him off-limits. Even a woman just looking for fun had to draw the line somewhere.

The table Jenny had spotted earlier was still empty, and she plopped down in a wooden chair facing the room. She grabbed a couple of kernels of popcorn from the basket on the table and looked around. Marcee stood at the bar, her face flushed and animated, a guy on each side. Mr. Tall Texan remained on the barstool, his gaze focused on the television screen.

The room was filled with men, but no one caught her eye . . .

Jenny's gaze froze. Two men stood in the doorway. Though they were both attractive, the guy on the left sent her pulse racing. Tall, dark, and exceedingly handsome. Even from a distance she could see that he had the kind of eyes a woman could get lost in.

His gaze searched the room with businesslike precision. By the way he scanned the tables, paying little attention to the occupants, it appeared sitting, rather than hooking up, was on his mind.

Those intense dark eyes reached Jenny's table, and suddenly it was too late to look away. His gaze traveled over her face and searched her eyes. The noise from the room faded, and Jenny's heart pounded an erratic rhythm. Staring was definitely bad manners. But Jenny couldn't take her eyes off him.

"Sorry I took so long."

Jenny wrenched her attention away from the man to find Marcee standing beside the table.

"I had a bit of trouble getting away." Marcee placed a glass of wine in front of Jenny and kept the bottle of beer for herself. "That Jake is quite a talker."

"Jake?"

"The guy who bumped into us," Marcee said. "Drove me crazy."

The disgust in Marcee's voice told Jenny everything she needed to know. "So he's out."

"Totally." Marcee took a long sip of beer. "One thing I can't stand is a man who loves to talk about himself."

Jenny chuckled. "Anyone ever tell you that you have impossibly high standards?"

"It's been a long time since anyone told me I had standards, much less impossibly high ones." Marcee laughed and took a sip of beer. "Anyway, forget about me. We have to find you a man. And not just any man. This guy has to be ready and willing and capable of meeting *all* your needs."

Jenny just smiled. Regardless of what Marcee thought, she hadn't come here with the intention of sleeping with anyone. Rather, her intention was merely to flirt and have fun. "That isn't what tonight is about."

"Sure it is. C'mon, pick a man, any man." Marcee waved a freshly manicured hand. Her wide, sweeping arc encompassed the entire bar.

Jenny's gaze scanned the room in spite of her determination not to give Marcee even the slightest bit of encouragement.

And, though she told herself that Marcee's suggestion was beyond ridiculous, Jenny couldn't stop herself from wondering—if she ever was crazy enough to engage in a one-night stand— whom she *would* pick.

Actually she didn't need to wonder. There was really only one contender in the entire bar. Jenny shifted her gaze and found the man from the doorway at a corner table. Casually dressed in jeans and a blue button-up shirt, he fit in with the sports-minded crowd. But though his eyes strayed to one of the television screens, he didn't seem caught up in the game like most of the guys.

He shifted his gaze and caught her staring again. She immediately looked away. A shiver of awareness traveled slowly up her spine. There was something about the guy. Something . . .

"Okay, who's it gonna be?" Marcee leaned close, her eyes bright and sparkly.

"No one." Jenny pulled her gaze from the stranger and shook her head, the lie flowing easily from her lips. "None of these guys are my type."

Marcee snorted in disgust. "We're not talking about someone you'd take home to meet your parents. We're talking about someone to f—"

Jenny clapped her hand over Marcee's mouth. "Must you be so graphic?"

Marcee pulled Jenny's hand away and grinned. "Sometimes I forget what a little prude you are."

Jenny bristled. "I am not a prude."

Marcee took a long drink from the bottle sitting in front of her. "Are too."

"Am not." The retort shot from Jenny's mouth before she could stop herself.

A knowing look filled Marcee's eyes, and she leaned forward in a confidential manner. "It's normal to feel scared. But it's like jumping off the high board. It gets easier after you do it once."

Jenny shot a quick glance at the table across the bar, strangely reassured to see the guy was still alone.

"I can't go home with someone I don't know." Contemplating having a drink and conversation with a stranger was wild and crazy enough for Jenny. "He could be a weirdo or have some disease."

Again her gaze drifted to the dark-haired man. He didn't look like a weirdo. He looked like a businessman out for the evening.

"People you've known for years can have a disease," Marcee said matter-of-factly. "That's why I carry these."

Marcee opened her bag and pulled out a handful of condoms.

Jenny stared at the variety of colorful squares spilling from Marcee's hand.

"Here, have some." Marcee dropped several

on the table, just as the waitress stopped to pick up the empty glasses.

The perky brunette's gaze flickered over the packets. She raised a finely arched brow. "Looks like someone has big plans for the evening."

When Marcee made no move to pick them up, Jenny snatched the foil squares and dropped them into her purse.

"Could I have another glass of wine, please?"

The waitress nodded, her eyes twinkling with amusement.

"Okay, so these might take care of the disease thing," Jenny said when the waitress was safely out of earshot. "But how do I know the guy isn't a sadistic killer?"

Instead of tossing off some flip comment, as Jenny expected, Marcee picked up her beer bottle and took a drink. After a long moment, she met Jenny's gaze, her expression suddenly serious. "You talk to him in a public place first. If you get even the slightest creepy feeling, you don't go with him."

Jenny's gaze drifted back to the guy at the table. He was staring down into his glass of beer. Despite the laughter and talk that surrounded him, the man appeared lost in his own thoughts.

She could empathize. Though Jenny had a

wonderful family and a slew of friends, she often felt isolated and alone.

Other than Marcee, her friends were into getting married and having babies. They hadn't understood her desire, her need, her drive to succeed. How could they? She didn't even understand it herself.

I bet he'd understand.

The thought should have surprised Jenny, but it didn't. Though they'd never exchanged so much as a single word, from the time their eyes had locked, she'd felt a connection.

"Inquiring minds want to know."

Marcee's words pulled Jenny back to the present. She furrowed her brow. "Want to know what?"

"Who's the lucky guy?" Marcee's voice resounded with barely contained anticipation. "Who are you going home with tonight?"

Three

Robert Marshall stared into the amber liquid. Coming here tonight had been a mistake.

He had no interest in being social, no time for such things.

So why had he come?

The question niggled at him. After all, he'd just gotten back from a business trip to Hong Kong on Wednesday and was still suffering from jet lag. The smart thing would have been to stay home, watch a few innings of the game, then go to bed early.

Alone.

The thought rose unbidden and Robert knew instinctively that's why he was here. After two years of working sixteen-hour days, he was tired of pretending that work was all he needed.

When Kyle had called and invited him out

barhopping, Robert had planned on an evening of beer, darts, and conversation. Looking for a woman hadn't even crossed his mind. But when Robert had walked through the front door of O'Malley's and seen the blond, he'd been surprised by the stirrings of desire.

She was pretty, rather than beautiful, with hair the color of honey and large eyes that looked blue, but might have been green. Slender, with curves in all the right places, she was really no different from all the other women in the place.

Until their gazes had locked. At that moment, Robert realized that eyes could indeed be a window into a person's soul. When their eyes met, even across the room, he'd seen the loneliness she hid so well from the world.

We have that in common.

"Robert."

He looked up. Kyle Rohren, his best friend since boyhood, stood next to the table. Robert had given Kyle a ride to the pub, but hadn't seen much of him since. Last he knew Kyle had been tossing darts with a woman he'd met soon after they'd arrived. And judging from the way the brunette was plastered against his friend's side, Kyle's evening was just beginning.

"Shellie invited me over to her place," Kyle said. "You're welcome to come."

Shellie marched her fingers up the front of Kyle's shirt. "A little postgame celebration."

Robert smiled. He might have been out of the social scene for a while, but even he could tell that three would be a crowd. "You two go ahead."

The woman tugged at Kyle's sleeve. "You heard the man."

Kyle pulled away, but softened the gesture with a smile. "Why don't you wait for me by the front door? I'll only be a minute."

"Ky-yle." Her bottom lip jutted out in a pout.

"It'll be just a minute." Kyle brushed a kiss across her lips and gently turned her toward the door. "I promise."

"Looks like someone can't wait to get you alone." Robert brought the glass of beer to his lips.

"What can I say?" Kyle pulled out a chair and sat down, as if he had all the time in the world. "Women see me. They want me. It's as simple as that."

Actually it wasn't far from the truth. Robert and Kyle had grown up together. Women had always flocked to the fun-loving Kyle. But for a reason that Robert had never fully understood, none of them kept Kyle's interest, at least not for long.

"You're a lucky man," Robert said with a smile.

Kyle's gaze slid to the brunette before returning to Robert. "How about I give Shellie the heave-ho and you and I check out that new club downtown?"

Although this was supposed to be a guys' night out, the last thing Robert wanted to do was put a damper on Kyle's evening. His gaze drifted to the table where the blond sat talking to her friend. "You go ahead. I'll be heading home as soon as I finish this beer."

Kyle followed his gaze. "She's pretty."

"I guess." Robert shrugged. "If you like blonds."

"Why don't you go over and say hello?" Kyle suggested, pushing his chair back and rising to his feet.

"Why don't you go meet your new girlfriend and mind your own business?" Robert shot a pointed glance to the doorway where Shellie now stood talking on her cellular phone.

"Better yet," Kyle said as if Robert hadn't even spoken, "take her home with you."

"Thanks for the great advice," Robert said with a hint of sarcasm. "But even if I wanted to, I'm not prepared."

Kyle's smile widened. He reached into his

pocket, pulled out a couple of foil packets, and tossed them on the table.

"No need to thank me." Kyle shot Robert a wink. "After all, what are friends for?"

"Are you sure you don't want to come?" Marcee cast a surreptitious glance at the doorway as if making sure Mr. Tall Texan was still waiting for her. "Iguana Joe's has great margaritas."

"I'm going to pass," Jenny said. "Once I finish this glass of wine, I'll probably just head home."

"You can't go home now." A shocked look crossed Marcee's face. "The bars won't close for another three hours."

Jenny just smiled and faked a yawn.

"How 'bout if I tell him to go on without me," Marcee offered. "You and I could hang out. The night is still young. There's plenty of time for you to find someone."

"I don't need a babysitter," Jenny said in a teasing tone. "Go on. Have fun."

Marcee's gaze slid around the still crowded bar. "Only if you promise, you'll have another drink and one more look around before you head home. There has to be someone here who trips your trigger."

Jenny resisted the urge to glance at the one

man who had already "tripped her trigger." "I promise. Now will you go?"

"You seem awfully eager to get rid of me." A speculative look filled Marcee's eyes. "I wonder why?"

Jenny forced a look of confusion. "I don't know what you're talking about."

Marcee's lips turned upward. "I think you've got your own plans for this evening. Plans you don't want to share."

"Marcee—"

"I'll go." Marcee pushed back her chair and stood. "But you better give me *all* the dirt tomorrow at work. What time are you going to be there?"

"The e-mail said Rich wanted us there by nine," Jenny murmured.

This Saturday was a special "team building" day thought up by Rich and some consultant he'd hired to boost morale. Jenny still hadn't made up her mind if she was going to show. Anyway, the last thing she wanted to think about was her job. Right now she had more pressing matters on her mind.

Jenny had lied when she'd told Marcee she planned to head straight home. She'd been biding her time, preferring not to have an audience in case she fell flat on her face.

Now there was no longer a reason to wait. It was time to make her move.

"Care if I sit down?" Surprisingly, the words came out low and sultry, just as Jenny had intended.

At the sound of her voice the man's head jerked up, and he shoved back his chair and stood.

"Please do." He met her gaze and smiled. After a moment his gaze dropped to the lacy camisole that clung to her curves.

Her skin prickled and a rush of desire, as unexpected as it was overwhelming, raced through her.

As he pulled out a chair for her, Jenny caught the faint scent of his cologne. It was a unique scent, smooth but spicy and very appealing.

And now that she stood close enough to touch him she saw his eyes weren't brown as she'd originally thought, but a strikingly brilliant blue.

Even as she sank into the chair, Jenny realized she'd made a mistake in approaching him. This guy was out of her league. Way too handsome to be interested in someone like her.

Not that she wasn't attractive, but he was gorgeous. Her hands tightened on the arms of the chair. On the count of three, she'd stand, make some excuse, and head for the door. One. Two. Thr—

"I noticed you the minute I walked in," he said. "You are by far the prettiest woman in the place."

A flush of pleasure traveled through Jenny at the unexpected compliment.

"I think someone has had too much beer," she finally managed to say with mock seriousness.

"This"—he gestured toward the mug—"is my first. And I meant every word I said."

The tension left her shoulders and the knot in her stomach unwound. She loosened her death grip on the chair arms. If he thought she was pretty, who was she to argue?

"I'm Robert Marshall," he said, extending a hand. "My friends call me Robert."

She laughed, but when he continued to hold her hand, the laughter died in her throat. Her eyes met his, and for a brief second Jenny could see her own desire reflected in the blue depths.

Embarrassed by the unexpected emotion, she looked away, thankful the dim light would hide the heat rising up her neck.

"And you are?" he asked after a moment.

"Jasmine," she said. "Jasmine Coret."

The minute the lie left her mouth, Jenny wondered what had gotten into her. Trying to emulate someone else was one thing, resurrecting the dead quite another.

"Coret?" Robert lifted a brow. "Are you French?"

Jenny took a sip of her wine and considered her options. She could tell Robert the truth and bore him to death. Or she could give Jasmine—and herself—another shot at life.

"My father is French." The lie tasted sweet on her tongue and flowed from her mouth like warm honey. "His family immigrated to the U. S. in the fifties when he was a boy."

"Parlez-vous français?"

Jenny's smile froze on her face. Lying was one thing, being foolhardy another. Although she'd taken the language in both high school and college, at the moment she could only recall some scandalous phrases Marcee had recently taught her. "Not really."

He smiled understandingly. "A second language is easy to lose if you don't use it. I take it your parents don't live in the area."

"They live in Phoenix." Hadn't her father said more than once last winter that he *wished* he lived in Phoenix? "How is it that you speak French?"

"I'm in Paris quite frequently for business," he said. "Being multilingual is a necessity if you do much international trading."

"Is that what you do?" Jenny asked. "International trading?"

"Among other things," he said. "How about you?"

Jenny thought for a moment. The last thing she wanted to talk about tonight was spreadsheets and tax charts.

"I'm a hairstylist." Jenny flashed a bright smile. It was a bit of a stretch considering she didn't even trim her own bangs, but her friend Kristy *had* opened a trendy salon and day spa in Highland Park last year and Jenny *had* helped with the business plan.

Robert took another sip of beer. "Do you like cutting hair?"

"There's a little more to the job than combs and scissors," she said in a teasing tone. Actually, helping Kristy had opened Jenny's eyes to all that was involved in running such a business. She'd been surprised to discover that dealing with hair was just a small part of Kristy's duties. "What I like most is the opportunity to be my own boss."

"Being your own boss isn't without risk," Robert said.

"I'm determined to be successful." Jenny leaned forward and spoke with unexpected fervor. "I've never been content with just getting by."

"You've definitely got the entrepreneurial spirit." Robert smiled, and her heart warmed at the approval in his eyes.

Jenny peered at his ruggedly attractive face through lowered lashes, her gaze drawn to his firm, full lips. What would it be like to kiss him?

God, it had been so long since she'd kissed a man, she wasn't sure she remembered how, and even longer since she'd . . .

Her throat grew dry and she swallowed hard.

The air crackled with electricity, and Robert's dark blue gaze locked with hers.

Kiss me.

A slow, sexy grin eased up the corner of his mouth, and for a second Jenny wondered if she'd voiced her desire aloud. But she couldn't ask because he leaned close, and suddenly she couldn't breathe, much less speak.

The noise of the bar faded and time stood still. He moved closer, so close she could feel the warmth of his body and inhale the spicy scent of his cologne. They were face-to-face, his mouth a mere heartbeat away.

An ache of wanting wrapped itself around Jenny, surprising her with its intensity. She breathed his name.

He paused and blinked, shaking his head slightly as if to clear it. His eyes took on a distant look, and when he sat back, Jenny knew she'd lost him.

Her heart fluttered like a trapped butterfly. She didn't know what had gone wrong, but she had the feeling the man sitting beside her was mere seconds away from getting up and walking out the door.

What would Jasmine do?

Men might walk out on Jennifer Carman, but no one would walk out on Jasmine Coret.

"Did I tell you I only started my business last year and it's already in the black?" It might not have been the topic Jasmine would have chosen to reel him back in, but Jenny didn't have much choice. She'd never been good at flirting, especially under pressure. But she could talk business anytime, anywhere.

He lifted a brow and the words continued to tumble from Jenny's lips, filling the uncomfortable silence. "Of course I researched the market and had a solid business plan before I even opened the salon. I realize such a venture might seem like small potatoes to you, but to be making money this early is quite an accomplishment."

Jenny paused for a breath and realized the faraway look had left Robert's eyes and he was now staring at her. She groaned inwardly. She'd always hated babblers and here she was babbling with the best of them. And *small potatoes*? Did anyone even use that term anymore? "Sorry. I didn't mean to bore you and go on about nothing."

"I wasn't bored." He suddenly smiled, and it was as if the sun had broken through the clouds. "I admire ambition."

A warm, fuzzy glow that had nothing to do with the alcohol she'd consumed washed over her. "You do?"

Robert nodded and sipped his beer. "I appreciate a woman who knows what she wants and is willing to work hard to get it."

"That's what I keep telling myself." Jenny leaned forward, forgetting she was only playing a part and that the business they were discussing wasn't really hers. "If I work hard, I'll succeed."

"Usually that's what happens." For a second the distant look returned to his eyes. "But sometimes things are out of our hands."

A momentary image of the e-mail flashed before her but Jenny shoved it aside.

"I try not to dwell on the negative," she said. "I have my goals, and I'm willing to do whatever it takes to meet them."

Just saying the words bolstered her morale and lifted her spirits. Despite her most recent setback, Jenny Carman wasn't down for the count. She was still a contender. She'd find a way to get back in the ring.

Robert finished his beer and motioned to the waitress. "What about having a family? Is that a goal?"

"That is so far down the road, it's not even on my radar," Jenny spoke from the heart, thinking of all she still wanted to accomplish. "Right now a husband and children would take too much time and just complicate my life."

"And a boyfriend?" he asked in an offhand tone.

"No time for that kind of relationship, either," Jenny said. "What about you?"

He shook his head and his gaze turned speculative. "You're really determined to fly solo?"

Jenny heaved an exasperated sigh. "Now you

sound like my father. If I was a man, he'd be ap-
plauding my successes instead of telling me I'm
going to regret the road I'm taking."

His gaze searched her face. "That has to hurt."

It was a simple statement, but so unexpected
and so close to the truth that Jenny had to blink
back tears. The last time she'd tried to talk to her
parents about her career had been a disaster.
Her mother had mentioned that Jenny's cousin
Mary Sue was now pregnant with her second
baby, and her father had told her to remember
that money didn't buy happiness. "It did."

Unexpectedly Robert reached over and gave
her hand a squeeze. And instead of immediately pulling away, she let his hand linger.

His touch sent a shiver up her spine, and all
sorts of crazy Marcee-type thoughts began dancing in her head.

After a long moment he spoke. "I don't care
what your father says; being in the black so
early is a major accomplishment and deserves
to be celebrated."

"You think we should celebrate?"

He nodded. "My friend Kyle was telling me
about a new club downtown. Good atmosphere,
great music. That's of course assuming you like
jazz . . . ?"

Jazz had never been something Jenny had

thought much about, one way or the other. She tried to ignore the red flags popping up in her head. Talking to the guy she'd just met in a bar was one thing, but to leave with him was something else entirely.

Still, tonight wasn't about following the tried-and-true but about experimenting.

"I'm not an expert, by any means," Jenny said with a lighthearted Jasmine-type laugh. "But I'd love to go with you."

Her lips lingered on the last two words, liking the sound of them on her tongue. Thanks to the decision to cast off her conservative Jenny-skin, she wasn't stuck spending another boring night alone.

She was with the most handsome man in the room and she was having fun.

Who could ask for anything more?

By the time they were ready to leave the club, two hours had passed, and Jenny didn't want the evening to end. They'd laughed and talked, and Jenny had been relaxed and spontaneous.

At one point they'd even discussed business theories. When Robert expressed surprise over the extent of her knowledge of accounting practices, Jenny had laughed it off and changed the subject to something lighter, determined to be more careful. Still, she'd enjoyed the dialogue.

Robert was a great conversationalist. Not to mention just one look from those intense blue eyes sent her heart into overdrive.

"Does your condo really overlook Lake Michigan?" Jenny asked, tracing an imaginary figure eight on the tabletop while they waited for the server to bring back Robert's credit card.

"The bedroom window has a great view of the lake," he said.

"I'd like to see it."

A startled look crossed his face. "Maybe you will," he said finally, offering her a noncommittal smile. "Someday."

Jenny knew with sudden certainty that day would never come. Though she'd had a wonderful time, it had quickly become apparent that they shared an obsession with work. He didn't have any more time for a relationship than she did. But tonight wasn't about relationships. It was about seizing the moment.

What would Jasmine do?

She met his gaze. "I've got time now."

The server returned and Robert slid the card into his pocket, an inscrutable look blanketing his face. Without a word, he extended his hand

to her. She automatically took it, the icy cold-
ness of her skin even more pronounced against
the warmth of his.

"Is it the view that interests you?" he asked
slowly. "Or the bedroom?"

Jenny was horrified by the bluntness of the
question. Jasmine just laughed. "I thought you
said the view was from the bedroom?"

"It is."

She smiled brightly. "Then I guess I'm interested in both."

"Even if tonight is all we have?" His gaze
remained steady on hers. Though his words
were sensible, his thumb massaging her palm
pushed sensibility to the bottom of Jenny's list
of considerations. "I can't promise more."

The cards were on the table. It was the moment of truth.

Jenny thought of how she'd been brought up,
the values her parents had instilled in her since
childhood. In her family, sex came after com-
mitment, after the wedding ring was on the
finger. Not before. And certainly not with a
stranger.

But Jenny didn't live in her parents' world. She
hadn't married in her early twenties and started
a family. She no longer dreamed of a white wedding and a house with a picket fence.

Jenny's gaze lingered on the man standing before her, patiently waiting for her answer. She searched his eyes and saw desire, hot and liquid, but also a heart-tugging uncertainty.

Her gaze flicked down to where his thumb drew a slow circle on her palm.

"Yes," she said, pulling their entwined hands to her mouth and pressing a kiss to the inside of his wrist. "Even if tonight is all we have."

Four

"So this is where you live." Jenny gazed up at the multistory building just off Navy Pier and tried not to gawk.

When Robert had said his condo was close to the lake, she never imagined he lived in one of the most exclusive complexes in the city.

"Home sweet home." Robert turned the Land Rover into the underground parking garage at the base of the modern cylindrical structure.

He pulled into a parking space, shut off the engine, and slanted a sideways glance. "Sit tight. I'll get the door."

Jenny smoothed the front of her skirt. Lake Michigan would look beautiful in the moonlight.

From his bedroom.

Her heart picked up speed and her smile was

slightly tremulous when he opened the door and offered her his hand.

As they walked to the lobby, Jenny's gaze couldn't help but be drawn to the man at her side . . .

She took in the width of his shoulders, the taut flatness of his stomach, and the way his jeans clung to his lean hips. He was a little over six feet of solidly muscled, incredibly good-looking male. And tonight he was all hers.

She sighed. While Marcee would feast on the guy for hours, Jenny wasn't sure what to do with him. Thankfully Jasmine wasn't worried at all.

Jenny felt the tightness in her shoulders ease.

The door to the lobby slid open as they approached, and an older black man lifted his gaze from the security monitors. "Evening, Mr. Marshall."

"Good evening, Harold," Robert said.

If Robert noticed the curiosity in the man's dark eyes when they settled on Jenny, it didn't show. Instead, with one hand resting easily at the small of her back, Robert steered her to the elevator. The dark cherrywood panels slid open the moment he pressed the button.

"Have you lived here long?" Jenny's gaze surveyed the beveled glass mirrors lining the elevator's walls, and she tried to ignore the heat she could feel coloring her cheeks.

"Two years." Robert followed her inside and hit the button for the fifteenth floor.

She expected him to elaborate, but instead he shoved his hands into his pockets and stood silently, rocking back on his heels.

Her irritation started to surge until she noticed the lines of strain edging his eyes and realized he was nervous, too.

Jenny took a deep breath. While she might not have Marcee's knack with men, she could certainly handle a little small talk.

"Did you buy your unit new?" she asked, deciding to bypass the weather.

"The building was about a year old when I moved here," Robert said. "The previous owner lived in New York and only used it when he was in town for business."

He'd stopped rocking back and forth. So far, so good.

"But it's your primary residence, right?"

Robert shrugged. "Since I'm gone a lot, it works."

Was that his way of warning her not to expect too much? Perhaps he was like those people she'd read about who had beautiful homes but not a stick of furniture inside.

The elevator slid to a stop, and Jenny told herself that no matter how simple the furnishings, she'd find something nice to say. And if she couldn't, she wouldn't say anything at all.

The moment he opened his door and Jenny caught a glimpse of the interior, she let out the breath she didn't realize she'd been holding. "Why, it's beautiful."

"It's okay." Robert tossed his keys on an entrance hall table.

It was more than okay. And more than beautiful. *Exquisite* was the word that came to mind, followed quickly by *breathtaking*.

The living room was a soothing shade of gray, and the stained ebony floor created a perfect background for the Tibetan rugs. It had a decided Art Deco feel, due in large part to the black-lacquer-and-silver table sitting in the middle of the living room. The table was huge—at least four feet in diameter—and everything in the room seemed to spin around it.

There were several abstract constructions, one that Jenny immediately recognized. "Is that a Sophia Vari?"

Robert nodded. "The one next to it is a Joel Shapiro."

"Are you a collector?" Jenny had developed a love of Art Deco art back in college, and Sophia Vari was one of her favorites. But she really did like the looks of the Joel Shapiro.

"Not really." Robert stared at the two wall hangings as if seeing them for the first time. "The designer thought they'd look good in here."

Disappointment coursed through Jenny, though she didn't know why it mattered whether he shared her love of Art Deco or not. After tonight she'd never see him again.

She glanced around the room looking for some personal touches that would give her insight into the man at her side.

She came up empty. The room was a work of art, as perfectly impersonal as any designer showroom.

"The living room overlooks the city." Robert dimmed the lights and pushed a button. The draperies parted silently.

He moved to her side, and they gazed out over the twinkling lights that made up downtown Chicago.

"That's the Sears Tower." He pointed. "And there's the John Hancock Building."

Jenny dutifully checked out the view. Despite having lived in Chicago her whole life, she had to admit the scene before her was spectacular. "Beautiful."

"Yes, you are."

The words were so soft that for a second she wondered if she'd only imagined them. Until she turned to find Robert gazing at her . . .

Her heart picked up speed, and she nervously brushed a stray piece of hair back from her face. "Is the rest of the place this nice?"

It was an inane comment, but with his gaze searing her skin she could barely talk, much less come up with something clever.

He studied her for a moment before his lips lifted in a slight smile. "I'll show you."

She followed him through a kitchen with the latest in appliances, a dining room with a Leleu table, and a library with a super-real painting that looked more like a window than a canvas.

"The bedroom is through here." He pushed open the door, and Jenny hesitated only a second before stepping inside.

As in the library, the walls of the master bedroom were upholstered in panels of dove gray. A sitting area was artfully arranged by the window. Once again Jenny searched the room for a personal touch. She came up blank again. The only sign of life was a suspense novel facedown on a mirrored side table . . . next to the bed.

Jenny moved to the window and stared out into the darkness. The enormity of what she was about to do hit her like a sledge.

She didn't know this guy. He didn't know her. Yet she'd pushed herself into his bedroom. For what? A disappointing roll in the hay? It was pure craziness to think she'd be able to respond to a stranger when ninety percent of the time she'd had to fake it with her former fiancé. The last time she'd made love, she'd been tentative and unsure, and Michael hadn't even been able to keep it up.

Jenny wrapped her arms around herself and shivered.

Robert joined her at the window, and his brow furrowed. "Are you cold?"

Jenny ignored the question and focused her gaze on the huge expanse of water stretched out before her. "The water looks positively frigid."

He didn't immediately respond, and when Jenny shifted her gaze back to him, she found him staring.

"I'm sure it's not frigid," he said softly.

Jenny flushed. "Looks can be deceiving."

"Not a chance." His gaze flickered downward and rested on her mouth for several seconds.

The brief glance touched Jenny like a heated caress, sending her pulse into double-time. Still, her fears remained. It had been so long since she'd been held, touched, caressed. She wasn't sure she'd be able to respond . . .

"How can you be so sure?" she asked.

Reaching out, Robert touched a single fingertip to her bare shoulder, then slowly dragged it down her arm. Goose bumps beaded her flesh, completely at odds with the inferno his feather-soft touch ignited.

"You are so sexy." Robert tucked a strand of hair behind her ear, his gaze dark and intense. "So very lovely."

"And you are so beautiful," she murmured.

A look of momentary surprise flashed in his blue eyes, and she realized with sudden horror what she'd said. "I meant handsome."

He tried not to smile, but the ever-so-slight lift of his lips gave him away.

He must think I'm an idiot.

Jenny groaned and turned away.

"Hey." With great gentleness, Robert turned her head back toward him.

"*Handsome* is such a bland word. I like *beautiful* much better." His gaze lingered on her face, and his eyes softened. "I especially like the way that word sounds on your lips. Say it again."

Jenny fought the urge to give in to her shyness. If she did, she knew the evening was over.

"Beautiful." She flattened her palm against his cheek and skimmed her thumb along his full bottom lip. She kept her gaze locked with his and licked her lips. "Gorgeous."

Capturing her hand in his, Robert turned it over and placed a kiss in her palm. Then he raised her hand to his lips and kissed the tips of each of her fingers. "Tonight I will make all your fantasies come true."

Something hot and intense flared in his eyes, and his gaze returned to her lips.

Her pulse seemed to stall, then thump like a bass drum. She stood frozen in place, her mind a blank except for the mantra pounding through it. *He's going to kiss me. He's going to kiss me.*

Mercifully he didn't make her wait. He slid his hand behind her neck and slanted his mouth against hers.

Jenny couldn't remember ever having been kissed quite like this before. It started out slowly but changed the moment Robert's tongue swept across her lips.

Her hands moved up, and she curled her fingers into the fabric of his shirt. She could feel the heat of his body under her hands, the steady thud of his heart.

Everything faded except the need to feel more of him. Taste more of him. Touch more of him.

Desire, hot and insistent and for so long forgotten, gushed through her, turning her insides to jelly. His hands slipped down to the small of her back and pulled her closer. His erection pressed against her belly, inspiring a dizzying myriad of sensual images of him, and her, together.

Jenny's fingers moved to the buttons of his shirt, and one by one they popped open.

The moon shone through the bedroom windows, bathing the room in a soft, pale glow. She could see the passion in his eyes and feel the heat that radiated from his body. He smelled of soap and some indefinable, warm male scent that made something tighten low in her abdomen.

Keeping his gaze firmly fixed on hers, Robert shrugged off his shirt. His pants quickly followed. In a matter of minutes he stood in front of her, clad only in black silk boxers. Though he was a businessman, he had a working man's body—corded with muscle, lean and tan. Dark hair converged on the flat planes of his stomach into a line that disappeared into the waistband of his shorts.

Broad shoulders, hard chest, lean hips. Robert Marshall was every woman's fantasy. Testosterone wafted from him like invisible tethers, tugging at Jenny, keeping her feet anchored to the floor.

"Now it's your turn," he said softly, his expression inscrutable, his gaze watchful.

Jenny reached behind her, her suddenly clumsy fingers searching for the elusive zipper.

"Allow me." Placing one hand on her shoulder, Robert spun her gently around. He eased the zipper down and, as she turned back toward him, the skirt floated to the floor, sliding sensuously over her body.

Would his hands be as soft against her skin? Or rougher? She shivered with anticipation. It was time she found out.

With uncharacteristic boldness, Jenny settled her hands on his hips and pulled him close, until their bodies touched from chest to knee. So close she could smell the lime in his aftershave. So close she could feel the heat from his body. So close she could see the flecks of gold in his eyes as his gaze swept across her body in an intimate caress.

Prickles of pleasure danced across Jenny's bare skin, and her heart thumped hard and fast. A wave of heat swept through her, gaining momentum at the desire simmering in his gaze.

He hadn't touched her and yet her flesh quivered.

"I'm beginning to think," Robert said, in a

husky, aroused voice, "that you're determined to have your way with me."

Jenny slanted him a decidedly Jasmine-like smile. "Would you mind?"

Something hot and sexy flared deep in Robert's blue eyes. "I'm all yours."

Jenny's heart skipped a beat. The way he was looking at her, with those sexy eyes all hot and focused, made her feel positively woozy.

"Yes," she said softly. "Tonight you're all mine."

She leaned forward and slowly traced a finger along his jaw and down his throat. The air crackled with intensity, and the flash of blue fire in his eyes made her pulse jump.

"I want to touch you," Jenny said in a sultry voice she barely recognized. "All over."

With a low groan, Robert pulled her down on the bed. His arms came around her; his mouth covered hers. She was completely surrounded by him. She reveled in the delicious feel of his body pressing against hers. In the warmth emanating from his skin. In the exquisite sensation of his tongue exploring her mouth.

Robert stroked long and slow and she threaded her fingers through his hair, instinctively kissing him back the same way. He consumed her mouth, and the taste of his want made her light-headed.

Jenny's heart thumped hard in her chest as her body came vibrantly alive. As they continued to kiss, she became bold, sliding her fingers across his chest, brushing the small bud of his nipple.

Robert's breath hissed between his teeth and his body jolted.

Tilting her head back, she watched his face as she repeated the caress. She smiled, reveling in her feminine power.

Jenny found his other nipple buried in the curling mat of hair and rubbed her thumb over the tight bud, the edge of her nail scraping ever so lightly.

"Yes . . ." he groaned, his voice thick with need.

She flicked the tip of her tongue over his earlobe, then ran it down the side of his neck. She nibbled. She nipped lightly with her teeth. She licked her way down his body, her tongue circling his nipple before taking it into her mouth.

A moan rushed past his lips. Sweat dampened his skin.

Reaching up, he grasped her arms and pulled her to him for an intimate, openmouthed kiss.

Jenny arched her head back, baring her neck

and throat to his lips, and a purr of pleasure rumbled in her throat.

Though she'd often heard it said that you couldn't miss something you never had, Jenny knew differently. She'd longed for this kind of passion her whole life.

His hand slid around her waist and flattened against her lower back, drawing her up against the length of his body.

Jenny's hips arched in instinctive invitation, her mind conjuring up images of naked limbs entwined . . . of Robert's strong body moving over hers, filling her, thrusting hard and deep.

Her hands moved to his back, skimming her fingertips across the smooth muscles.

"The way you smell drives me crazy," he said, nuzzling her hair, kissing her neck.

"The way you feel." He slid his hands over the smooth silk of her camisole before pushing aside the skimpy lace and cradling her breasts in his wide palms.

He caught her nipples between thumb and forefinger, plucking not quite gently. Intense pleasure hovering on the knife edge of pain shot though Jenny, and her breath caught on a moan.

Please don't stop.

A second later Jenny realized she'd been foolish to worry. Robert slipped the camisole over her head and without missing a beat, buried his face in the soft fullness.

His tongue lapped one taut nipple, teasing it to aching hardness before taking it into his mouth. She swallowed another moan, her pulse hammering in her ears.

Robert lingered over her breasts, licking and suckling, in no apparent hurry to move on. Jenny squirmed beneath him, her nails digging into his strong shoulders.

Just when Jenny thought she'd die from the pleasure, his hand slipped downward to the part of her that was already swollen with need. She lifted her hips and Robert tugged off her panties, kissing along the way, nipping with his teeth, driving her crazy.

When his eyes met hers, Jenny saw the reflection of her own want and need reflected in the dark and hungry gaze. His fingers played over her lightly, separating soft, damp folds, stroking tender flesh while he kissed her with an erotic intensity that had her reeling.

Jenny opened her legs to the gentle, persistent pressure, and he slipped a finger inside.

She gasped and grabbed on to him even as her muscles contracted around him.

"You're tight." Robert kissed her hot and

hard. "And wet." He moved his lips to her ear, and whispered, "That's good."

Her arms tightened convulsively around him, all her earlier hesitation burned away in the heat building between them. Jenny's lips sought his and she drank him in. But it still wasn't enough.

"I want you," Jenny whispered against his throat, breathless and impatient. "Inside me."

Robert made a low, guttural sound and hurriedly shed his boxers.

Jenny's gaze took in the length of him, and a ripple of excitement skittered up her spine.

He quickly unwrapped the condom he'd tossed on the bedside stand and then he was inside her, filling her, hard and firm. The sheer bliss was so intense, so startling, Jenny knew it was only a matter of a few strokes before she'd come.

She arched her hips, rocking against him, taking all he had to give. She captured his mouth in a deep, hot, tongue-tangling kiss that mimicked the fast, hard, frantic mating of their bodies. Her body trembled, and she fought the orgasm building inside her, not wanting it to be over.

But she couldn't hold on. He pumped his hips forward and back, again and again, every thrust heavier and harder than the one before until she cried out, her nails clawing his back, her body convulsing around his shaft, milking him, shuddering with the force of her own release.

Five

Jenny rolled over and opened her eyes. For a second she wasn't sure where she was until she saw her clothes on the floor and realized she was naked beneath the silky smoothness of the sheets. Images of the night flooded back in a rush.

She stretched and couldn't help but smile. Last night a stranger had made her feel like a woman. Something her former fiancé hadn't been able to do in all the years they were together.

"Good morning."

Jenny turned with a start and found Robert propped up on one elbow, staring at her breasts.

"I wondered when you'd wake up." His lips curved upward.

Her nipples hardened beneath his gaze, and for a second, the old Jenny surfaced, urging her to jerk the sheet over her head. But that was the sexually frustrated Jenny. The one with all the unfulfilled needs. Not the woman she'd been last night, the one who was bold and sassy and liked a man's eyes on her.

"Good morning yourself." Impulsively Jenny lifted her head and kissed him on the mouth.

His lips were warm, smooth, and simply delectable. She lingered an extra heartbeat, savoring the taste, and then laid her head back on the pillow.

Surprise followed by desire flashed in his eyes.

"I wasn't sure you'd still be here," he said.

Jenny's smile froze on her lips. Had she broken some unwritten etiquette rule by sleeping in? Should she have hopped up out of bed, pulled on her clothes, and slipped out the door before he'd awakened?

That seemed a bit extreme—not to mention rude. Surely this was more the Emily Post way of handling the situation; hot sex followed by polite conversation.

Or maybe hot sex followed by polite conversation followed by even more hot sex?

Anticipation skittered up her spine. Jenny leaned close, letting her breast brush against his arm. "What did you have in mind?"

"A shower," he said breezily. "Then breakfast."

Disappointment replaced anticipation. Though they'd awakened during the night and made love, Jenny had hoped for a repeat performance this morning. But making love three times in eight hours was probably expecting a lot out of any man. Heck, she'd practically had to beg Michael to do it three times a *week*.

Jenny stifled a sigh, feeling somehow cheated that the wild and crazy ride had so quickly come to an end.

Jasmine would never let the morning end in such a civilized manner.

Not when there was still time for more.

"A shower sounds like fun." The words sounded light and flirtatious, just as she'd intended. "I assume you'll be joining me?"

"Into conserving water?"

She winked, encouraged by the flare of heat in his gaze. "Something like that."

Robert pulled her close, and Jenny couldn't help but snuggle against him for a moment, liking the feel of his strong arms around her.

"This is nice," Robert said with a contented sigh.

"I had a good time last night," Jenny said, her

fingers playing with the thick mat of curls on his chest.

"Actually it was quite outstanding." He stroked her hair with the tips of his fingers. "Très magnifique in fact."

A rush of feminine pride washed over her. Last night she'd given as good as she got. Not once had she let her shyness interfere. And she'd been able to be so reckless and unabandoned because of Robert's openness. Finally she'd found a man who wasn't constrained by silly do's and don'ts of proper behavior in bed. One who liked to explore . . .

His hand slid down the length of her body, leaving a trail of heat in its wake.

"After we shower," he said in a deep, sexy voice that sent a shiver up her spine, "I'd like to make you breakfast. That is, if you have time."

"Time?" The feel of his hand against her skin brought back all sorts of sensations and desires, not one of which had anything to do with schedules or food.

"I didn't know if you needed to be at the salon this morning."

Jenny frowned. Her brows drew together. Why would she need to be at a salon?

You told him you were a hairstylist, the tiny voice inside whispered, *and that you owned a day spa.*

For a second guilt niggled at her, but she shoved the emotion aside and forced a bright smile. "I hadn't planned on going in today."

"Excellent." He rolled over and stood. "Then we won't rush."

"Rush?"

"Showers, when done properly," he said, reaching down and pulling Jenny to her feet, "take a lot of time."

"Shower sex is the best." A dreamy look crossed Marcee's face and she inhaled deeply. "There's nothing like the feel of a man's hand sliding soap across your bare skin."

As Marcee droned on, Jenny wondered what had ever possessed her to tell her friend the truth about her daring adventures with Robert.

Of course, Marcee had known something was up when Jenny had slipped into work four hours late. Still, Jenny could just as easily said she'd overslept.

"When are you seeing him again?"

Jenny blinked and pulled her thoughts back to the present. "I'm not."

Shock followed by disbelief skittered across Marcee's perfectly made-up face. She leaned forward and rested her elbows on the desk. Though they were alone in Jenny's tiny office,

Marcee's voice lowered to a deep-throated whisper. "That doesn't make sense. You told me the sex was great."

"It was." Jenny kept her tone casual. "But we agreed up front it'd be just a one-night thing."

Still, she couldn't help being piqued that he hadn't asked to see her again. As Jasmine, she'd thrown her inhibitions to the wind and let him fulfill her fantasies. Maybe that was the problem. Maybe she hadn't worked hard enough to fulfill *his* fantasies.

"Everyone always says that. It's just a way out." Marcee's brow furrowed. "Was he a jerk or something?"

Jenny shook her head.

"He's married." The words burst from Marcee's lips and a look of triumph crossed her face. "That's why you're not seeing him again."

For a fraction of a second, Jenny was too stunned to speak. But once she had a chance to consider Marcee's suggestion, the thought was so ridiculous, Jenny had to laugh. "No way."

Marcee's gaze narrowed suspiciously. "Are you sure?"

Jenny understood Marcee's skepticism. At work Jenny had a reputation for always seeing the glass as half full, for believing the best about people. But that didn't mean she wore blinders. She'd scoped out Robert's condo and found no womanly influence. No feminine toiletries in the bathroom cabinet, no extra clothes in the bedroom closet. "Positive."

"He's not married or a jerk. He's great in bed and handsome as sin." Marcee lifted a perfectly arched brow. "Yet you aren't seeing him again?"

"One night was all it was supposed to be." Jenny wiped suddenly damp palms against her skirt. "Besides I'm busy. Steve's promotion came out of left field. I need to figure out a new battle plan. I don't have time—"

"Puh-leeze." Marcee rolled her eyes. "There's *always* time for sex."

"I'm busy. Robert is busy." Jenny's voice rose despite her best efforts to control it. "Why is that so hard to understand?"

Marcee stared at Jenny for a long moment, her expression inscrutable. "Remember when you were on that cheesecake kick?"

Jenny relaxed against the back of her chair. She breathed a sigh of relief. A sudden switch in topics was a well-known Marcee phenomenon. Normally it drove Jenny crazy. But this time she welcomed the change.

Visions of raspberry cheesecake danced before her eyes. For some women, chocolate was their stress buster. For her, it was cheese-cake.

"Jenny?"

Jenny pulled her thoughts back to the present and realized Marcee was waiting for a response. "Of course I remember. I was on a first-name basis with the takeout person at the Cheesecake Factory."

"Wasn't that when you were working on that audit from hell? The one way out in Wauke-gan?"

Jenny nodded. She could feel her blood pressure rise at the mere mention of the crazy client she'd worked so hard to please.

"You weren't even close to a Cheesecake Factory."

Jenny smiled ruefully. "I'd have driven a hundred miles if I'd had to."

"That's what I'm talking about." Marcee poked Jenny's arm with her finger. "It wasn't convenient but you did it anyway. Having that piece of cheesecake was important to you."

All the puzzle pieces suddenly clicked into place. Jenny groaned. Why did Marcee have to play the wise sage today of all days? "Don't tell me you're comparing cheesecake to sex?"

"Think about it." Marcee's expression was surprisingly serious. "No matter how busy we are, we make time for what's important. Whether that's cheesecake . . . or sex."

"So you're saying if I can walk away from sex with Robert, he must not be that important to me." Reassured that her tone remained steady, Jenny continued, "And if he can walk away, I must not be that important to him. Is that right?"

Marcee took a long sip from her Diet Coke and gazed at Jenny over the top of her can. "You tell me."

"I'd have found a way to fit him into my schedule." Jenny tried for nonchalance, but just as the words were coming out, something happened in her throat and her voice broke. "He wasn't interested. Imagine that. A man not interested in me."

Jenny twisted her mouth in a semblance of a smile. Her eyes were dry—she'd never cry in front of Marcee—but inside, she felt desolate. When she and Robert made love, she believed he'd felt the connection. But if that were true, he'd have wanted to see her again, despite making that deal.

"I'm not an experienced lover," Jenny said, surprising herself by voicing the fear. "He probably thought I was a big dud."

A corner of Marcee's mouth lifted in a faint

smile. "I don't think he'd have gone for the repeat performances—as in plural—if you'd been a dud."

As comforting and ego-boosting as that possibility was, Jenny had already considered and discarded it. Robert, after all, was highly sexual. No man could make love like that without lots of experience. More than likely he'd just decided to make the best of the evening.

"Maybe he thought he'd be kind and see if I improved with practice," Jenny said.

"Kind?" A choking laugh erupted from Marcee's lips.

Jenny pursed her lips together. "It doesn't matter."

"Did he ask for your number?" Marcee probed, obviously determined to ferret out every last detail.

"Yes," Jenny reluctantly admitted. "But just to fill the awkward silence when we were saying good-bye."

"He might surprise you." Marcee's red-lacquered fingernail circled the top of her Diet Coke can. "Busy or not, Jenny Carman isn't going to be that easy for him to forget."

"Actually," Jenny said, "if Robert does call, he'll be expecting to talk to Jasmine Coret, not Jenny Carman."

"Jasmine Coret?" Marcee's brows pulled together. "Do I know her?"

Jenny didn't blame Marcee for being confused. When she'd relayed the events of last night to Marcee earlier, she'd deliberately left off the pretending-to-be-another-person part.

"Jasmine was a friend of my grandmother. She died when she was about my age." Jenny traced a figure eight on the desktop with her finger. "Last night I . . . well, you could say I . . . resurrected her."

"This sounds interesting." Marcee sat up straight. "Tell me more."

"Robert thinks I'm live-for-the-moment Jasmine." Jenny still couldn't believe she'd pulled it off. Robert had no idea she was a dull accountant who had trouble talking to men. "He's also under the impression that I own a salon and day spa in Highland Park."

Marcee tilted her head, a bemused look on her face. "And why would he think that?"

Jenny smiled sheepishly. "Because that's what I told him."

Marcee squealed. "You made up a whole new persona?"

Jenny dipped her head slightly.

"I didn't think you had it in you." Admiration filled the redhead's eyes, and Jenny sensed that not only had she surprised Marcee by the admission, she'd moved up a notch in her friend's estimation.

For a second, Jenny basked in her friend's approval. She should have known she couldn't shock Marcee. After all, there wasn't much her friend hadn't done or seen.

"I liked being Jasmine," Jenny admitted.

"Jasmine." Marcee nodded approvingly. "It has an exotic, free-spirited sound."

"It's hip and cool." Jenny smiled, remembering again how confident she'd felt as the irrepressible woman. "Not boring, like Jenny."

Her friend didn't argue. She'd told Jenny often enough that her name made her sound sweet and pure. Coming from Marcee, that was definitely no compliment.

Marcee took another long sip of her diet soda. "So what's next?"

"What do you mean, what's next?"

"You resurrected the woman," Marcee said. "Surely you're not going to let her die again."

"That's exactly what I'm going to do."

"Don't be so hasty. Consider the possibilities." Marcee's eyes snapped with excitement. "Jasmine could be your alter ego. She could open up a whole new world to you."

Instead of immediately dismissing the idea

as she once might have done, Jenny took a few moments to mull over the suggestion.

"I could make a list," Jenny said, almost to herself. "Write down all the crazy things I've thought about doing but never had the guts to do."

"That's the spirit." Marcee's voice resonated with barely contained excitement. "It'll be so much fun. You're already off to a great start."

Marcee's enthusiasm was contagious. Jenny pulled a pad of paper from her desk drawer along with a pencil. She wrote the number one before tossing her pencil down on the desktop. "This is nuts. I'm not going to be able to do these things."

Marcee picked up the pencil and offered it to Jenny.

"This isn't just about you," Marcee said, her expression surprisingly serious. "It's about Jasmine. About her spirit, her hopes, her dreams. This may be her only chance to live out those dreams."

And though Marcee didn't elaborate, they both knew it might be Jenny's only chance as well.

Jenny took the pencil and began to write.

Six

"I can't believe I'm here." Jenny glanced around the foyer of the large home in Lake Forest and took a sip of champagne.

If Marcee hadn't gotten a call about a party honoring a local rock group who'd just signed with a major label, Jenny knew she'd probably be spending another Saturday night cleaning her closets.

When she'd put "crash a party" as one of the items on her "Jasmine list," Jenny had envisioned sneaking into an event honoring a visiting dignitary, not one where almost every guy had hair as long as hers and the girls looked like they'd just stepped off the set of an MTV video.

"This party is the best." Marcee lifted a bottle of imported beer to her lips. "Lots of action and not a lot of security."

The last part wasn't entirely true. Security

guards had been turning away lots of men—
and women, too—when Jenny and Marcee had
arrived at the gate. That's when Jenny discovered Marcee knew the lead singer for Mellon.
Apparently she and Ric were "intimately" ac-
quainted.

Since she and Marcee weren't on the guest
list, the guards had to call for the okay. But they
were more than willing. Probably because one
of them seemed particularly taken with Marcee's cleavage. Or maybe it was her friend's
short skirt that made him so cooperative.

Of course Marcee wasn't the only hottie. Jenny
wore a fashionable tunic dress in cream and gold
stripes. The V-neck hinted at curves, but what
made Jenny feel sexy tonight was what couldn't
be seen.

When Marcee had perused Jenny's list, she'd
suggested combining numbers three and fifteen. So Jenny—or rather, Jasmine—had not
only crashed a party, she'd done it leaving her
sexy undies at home.

It was odd, Jenny thought, how such a simple
thing as not wearing any underwear could
make her feel daring and Jasmine-like.

"C'mon." Marcee jerked her arm. "There's
dancing outside."

The pounding bass grew louder the closer

they got to the pool. Surprisingly Jenny didn't mind the noise. The music had a hypnotic rhythm that made her want to let go of her inhibitions. But, other than Marcee, Jenny didn't know a soul. Whom would she dance with?

Once outside, Jenny realized she needn't have worried. Other than a few couples grinding, the poolside was a mass of individuals caught up in the riotous beat.

Jenny lost track of Marcee in a matter of minutes. But instead of wasting time searching for her friend, Jenny had a second glass of champagne and socialized. Surprisingly relaxed, she soon found herself dancing beside people she didn't know and singing along to songs she barely recognized.

When her head started to spin and her shoes began to pinch, Jenny grabbed a beer from a passing waiter, plopped down in the first empty deck chair she saw, and kicked off the heels.

"I should've known I'd see you here."

The familiar voice sent a shiver up Jenny's spine. She turned her head.

Next to her, dressed casually in khaki shorts and a cotton T-shirt—and looking more like a college student than a successful businessman— sat last night's one-night stand.

The beer, which had been sliding down smooth as silk, took a wrong turn. Jenny gasped and began to cough.

Taking the napkin Robert held out to her, Jenny swiped at her watering eyes. She took her time, using the extra seconds to regain her composure. Her heart had leaped to her throat at the sight of him. But Jenny had her pride. No way would she do or say anything that would make her appear desperate.

After all, she wasn't some pathetic accountant that could only expect to be used as a booty call for a gorgeous man like Robert. She was sexy, confident Jasmine Coret.

With that thought firmly in mind, Jenny took a deep breath, plastered a sassy smile on her face, and pointed her beer bottle at Robert. "Are you following me?"

Robert just laughed and dropped his gaze from her face to her dress. "You look great. Very pretty."

Normally Jenny would have blushed. Instead she brought the bottle to her lips and took a long drink, determined to project a cool confidence. Still, she couldn't help the liquid heat that pooled low in her belly at the smoldering desire in his eyes.

"I didn't know you liked beer," he said when the silence lengthened.

"There's a lot about me you don't know." More than a little light-headed, Jenny leaned back in her chair and decided mixing wine and beer had been a mistake.

"Are you a fan of the group?" Robert asked.

Jenny crossed her legs, and his gaze followed her movement. Her breasts tingled, and an ache took up residence between her legs. "What group?"

"Mellon," he explained patiently. "This is their party."

That's right, Jenny thought. Marcee had slept with the lead singer. "I'm a big fan."

"Jake Marshall, the drummer, is my cousin." Robert shook his head, and the dimple in his cheek flashed. "His parents didn't think he had talent. I guess he showed them."

Jenny wondered if Jake was as hot as his cousin. It didn't seem possible. Who could top Robert? Robert, whose hair curled in sexy little wisps just above his collar. Robert, whose eyes were the color of the sky. Robert, whose lips were mere inches from hers.

Leaning forward, Jenny trailed a finger down his cheek. "You know, you really are a foxy hunk."

Robert's lips twitched. "How much have you had to drink?"

Jenny tilted her head, pulling her brows together. Was he insinuating she was drunk? She hadn't had *that* much to drink. Two or three glasses of champagne. A beer. Or was it two?

Considering numbers were her business, it struck her as funny that she couldn't seem to come up with a definitive count. An accountant shouldn't have trouble counting to four or five. Jenny swallowed a giggle and shrugged.

"C'mon. I'll take you home." Robert rose and held out his hand, his intense gaze heating the bare skin beneath her cotton dress. And by the look in his eyes he liked what he saw.

Now this was more like it . . .

But as much as Jasmine wanted to hop back into bed with him, Jenny decided to make him wait. Instead of taking his hand, she took another sip of beer and said the first thing that popped into her head. "I think I'm going to call you Superman."

Apparently realizing that getting her to leave wasn't going to be easy, Robert sat back down, and an indulgent smile tipped his lips. "You're not making sense."

"X-ray vision." Jenny tapped a finger against

her temple. "You can see through my dress that I'm not wearing any underwear."

"Your conversations are always so interesting."

Jenny turned toward the amused masculine voice. A blond-haired man who looked vaguely familiar crouched down next to her chair.

The man slanted a sideways glance at Robert before turning back to Jenny and holding out his hand. "Kyle Rohren. Ordinary guy. No super powers. But if you show me your naked body, I'll show you mine."

Jenny took the man's hand and gave him a once-over that normally she'd have never pulled off without blushing. The champagne was making her bold, and she liked the feeling. "Robert and I got naked. He didn't ask to see me again."

The shocked look on Robert's face made her giggle.

Kyle shifted his gaze to Robert. "You've been holding out. You didn't say a word about a one-night stand with this lovely lady."

"It was not a one-night stand," Robert said firmly.

"You say tomato." Jenny's hand fluttered in the air. "I say toe-mah-toe."

Whatever he wanted to call it, the fact remained that after a fabulous night—and morning—of sex, he hadn't asked to see her again. Clearly, he hadn't liked her as much as she'd liked him.

Time to move on, Jenny murmured to herself.

"What?" Robert asked.

Time to get my mind off you.

Jenny cleared her throat and smiled brightly at Kyle. "Care to dance?"

"I'd love to dance," Kyle said. "Or get naked. Your choice."

When Jenny had to resist the urge to giggle again, she realized the alcohol must be affecting her more than she realized. Before tonight she hadn't giggled since fifth grade.

"Too bad you're leaving." Robert cast a pointed glance at his friend, then shifted his gaze back to Jenny. "I'm afraid you're stuck with me."

Kyle opened his mouth, but the look on Robert's face must have reminded him of where he needed to go. Still, he took a moment to grab Jenny's hand and bring it to his lips. "It was a pleasure meeting you. I hope we see each other again real soon."

Jenny sighed as he disappeared into the crowd. Though Kyle didn't make her heart beat the slightest bit fast, he'd seemed like a good guy. "What nice manners."

Robert snorted. "Kyle's a real gentleman."

There was an edge to the words, and Jenny got the feeling that at the moment Robert didn't like his friend much. But it didn't matter. After tonight she probably wouldn't see either of them again. Suddenly, unexpectedly, a dark cloud settled over her, and tears pushed against the backs of her lids.

But Jenny wasn't about to get all weepy and maudlin. This was Jasmine's night to shine and Jenny's night to have some fun. She blinked the moisture back, slipped on her shoes, and stood. "C'mon, handsome. Time to grind. It's on my list."

"List?"

"Something I've always wanted to do." Jenny grabbed his hand and pulled him to his feet.

The dark and sensual rhythm stirred Jenny's blood, and against her better judgment, she looped her arms around Robert's neck. Stiff and awkward at first, Jenny took all of fifteen seconds to lose herself in the music.

She shoved her pelvis forward, and his hardness strained against her with every swivel of her hips. They were as close as they could possibly be with their clothes still on.

Beads of perspiration dampened her skin, and her heart raced. Waves of longing washed over her. If she closed her eyes she could almost believe they were making love again . . .

"Come home with me," Robert's deep voice whispered against her ear. His hand slid up her side, his thumb stopping just under her breast. "I'm going to be leaving tomorrow. I want to spend some time with you."

Heat sluiced through Jenny and she responded by planting an openmouthed kiss on his neck. He responded by dragging his thumbnail across the tip of her nipple. The groan had barely left her lips when a firm hand closed over her shoulder and jerked her from his arms. Outraged, Jenny whirled.

Marcee stood with her hands on her hips, her green eyes flashing. With her smeared lipstick and disheveled hair, Marcee looked like she'd just hopped out of bed. But this wildcat wasn't purring with satisfaction.

Concern flowed through Jenny. "What happened?"

"Ric's a jerk. Success has gone to his head." A tiny muscle jumped in Marcee's jaw. She glanced at Robert before shifting her gaze back to Jenny. "I'm leaving. You coming?"

Jenny hesitated only a second. "Of course."

Turning to Robert, Jenny experienced a pang of regret. She placed her hand against his cheek, and his eyes darkened. Giving in to temptation, Jenny kissed him hard on the mouth. One last time.

Jenny handed the man at the counter her credit card and stared down at the belly button ring visible above the waistband of her skirt. She couldn't believe she'd finally had the nerve to do it. When the guy had pushed the needle through her skin she'd almost fainted. But she was happy she'd stuck it out. Sure it had hurt— more than she'd ever imagined—but having the shiny ring with the faux emerald made her feel young, carefree . . . and sexy.

And she had Jasmine to thank. After the success she'd enjoyed at the party, she'd been determined to continue with her list. Monday morning she'd confronted Rich about the promotion going to Steve. She'd made it clear that unless she got a promotion she was going to look for another job. Though he'd insisted he didn't want her to leave, he hadn't made her a manager. That's when Jenny had added "find a fun accounting job" to her Jasmine list.

She'd made a few phone calls that afternoon and scored a next-day interview at the corporate offices of Kyllie's, a popular clothing firm that had been recently featured in *Cosmo*.

Bright and early this morning, Jenny had called in sick. Though she'd pleaded guilty to a migraine, "pampered princess" was really the name of today's game plan. After a manicure and pedicure, she'd had her hair razor cut and peanut-butter-colored highlights added. Then she'd headed downtown for some serious shopping. After buying some trendy—and obscenely expensive—fashions, she'd walked into State Street Body Piercing Salon.

Most of the people Jenny knew who had piercings had done them while in college. At thirty, she was way behind the curve. Her parents had always viewed tattoos and body piercing as the ultimate rebellion. Even after she'd grown up, Jenny had deferred to their wishes on these issues. Until now.

She stared at the clerk as he rang up the service. With hair down to his shoulders and a Fu Manchu mustache, he couldn't be more different from Robert. But there was something about the guy that reminded her of him. As she signed the credit card slip, she decided it must be his eyes. They were a bright vivid blue.

The kind of eyes a girl could drown in.

"Ma'am," the man said. "Your card."

Jenny realized that while she'd been staring, the guy had been standing there holding out

Cindy Kirk

her Visa. She took the card and dropped it into her purse.

He smiled and gave her a wink.

Jenny would have blushed. Jasmine shot him a wink of her own.

"Have a great day," she said with an airy wave.

Though she loved the outfit she had on, Jenny had brought a suit and a pair of pumps to wear for the interview. Her friend who worked at the Palmer House Hotel had said she could use an empty room for a quick change. She just hoped the skirt would stay on because there was no way she could zip it all the way up. Her piercing hurt like crazy.

Because the hotel was five blocks in the opposite direction, Jenny knew she'd have to hurry if she hoped to make it there and back to Michigan Avenue in time for her interview.

Shoving open the door, Jenny barreled out of the shop intent on doing some serious power walking. She'd barely gone three steps when she slammed into a rock-hard chest.

She fell backward, but strong arms reached out to steady her. "I'm so sorry," she said. "I wasn't loo—"

The words died on her lips. Her skin turned to gooseflesh.

Robert smiled. His hands lingered for a moment longer before dropping to his side. "What a pleasant surprise."

Jenny cast a quick glance from Robert, resplendent in a navy suit, to the distinguished-looking man at his side.

The silver-haired man's gaze settled briefly on Jenny before moving to the slim gold watch at his wrist. "Robert, I've got a meeting at four. Call me tomorrow and we'll finalize the figures."

The man turned to go but Robert grabbed his arm. "Wait a minute, Bill," he said. "I want you to meet a friend of mine."

Robert laid a familiar hand on her shoulder. "Jasmine Coret, this is Bill James, one of my business associates."

Jenny shifted her shopping bags to one hand and shook Bill's hand with the other.

A quizzical look filled the man's eyes. "Have we met before?"

She studied him for a moment before she made the connection. Bill was one of Rich Dodson's buddies. She'd been introduced to him several years ago at a charity fund-raiser at the Westin.

"I don't think so," Jenny said, her smile never wavering. "Unless maybe I've cut your hair? I run a salon and day spa in Highland Park."

The lines between Bill's brows deepened. He shook his head. "No, that's not it."

"I seem to have one of those faces everyone thinks they've seen," Jenny said with a little laugh. A curious thrumming filled her body. She should be quaking in her shoes. Instead, she'd never felt more alive. Adrenaline surged and her mind snapped to high alert.

Coming clean with Robert—if she ever saw him again—about her identity had been number two on her list. Now Jenny realized she didn't want the game to end. She was having too much fun being Jasmine. Way more fun than she'd ever had as herself.

After exchanging a few pleasantries, Bill hailed a cab and Jenny was left alone with Robert. She looked up to find his gaze focused on the exposed skin between her skirt and shirt, a puzzled look on his face.

"I don't remember you having your belly button pierced."

"It's been a long time since you've seen me naked," Jenny said, gazing up at him through lowered lashes. "It's easy to forget things."

"It's only been four days." Robert's gaze dropped back to her midriff, heating the skin.

"I explored every inch of your body. There was no ring in your belly."

Jenny's choice was to blush or laugh. She chose the latter. "Okay, you win. I just had it done."

He leaned forward, and his eyes widened at the sight of the angry, red skin surrounding the ring.

"It looks sore," he said. "But definitely sexy."

"No pain, no gain," Jenny said with an impish smile.

He straightened, and his gaze met hers. "You did something different with your hair."

"I'm a hairstylist." Jenny lifted a shoulder in a shrug. "We change our look all the time."

She was impressed with herself. The comeback had sprung to her lips almost without her thinking. This Jasmine role was really becoming natural.

"Very stylish," Robert said. "You look fabulous."

A warm rush of pleasure stole over her. She'd spent her life not hearing many such compliments, and she could easily stand here all day and soak them in. But she had to go. Forget the Palmer House. Forget changing clothes. If she didn't start putting one foot in front of the other right now, she'd be late for the interview.

"It's been great seeing you," Jenny said. "But I need to run. I've got an appointment at four-thirty."

"Where are you headed?" he asked.

"Down on Michigan," she said being deliberately vague.

"I'll walk with you," Robert said.

"Are you headed in that direction?"

"I am now." He smiled, showing a mouthful of perfect white teeth. "Let me carry those."

Without giving her a chance to answer, Robert took the shopping bags from her hands and they began to walk.

"They're heavy—" she protested.

The dimple in his cheek flashed. "I think I can manage."

Jenny's mouth went dry. Dear God. Handsome as sin and a gentleman as well. No wonder she'd hopped into his bed so quickly. No wonder she wanted to hop back there again.

But she couldn't think about that now. As much as she wanted him, she wanted this job more. Jenny picked up the pace.

"So, how's business?"

"Business?"

"The salon?"

"Um," Jenny hesitated. "Good. It's great. Booming, actually."

"I've been meaning to call you—"

Jenny laughed. She wasn't sure exactly why, it just came out.

His brows pulled together.

"I want to see you again," he said firmly, emphasizing each word, his gaze riveted to hers. "Unless you don't want to see me . . ."

What was there about this man? The liquid blue of his eyes tugged at her, pulling her from the solid shore toward a place where she could be over her head in seconds.

Jenny slowed her pace and stopped in front of the John Hancock Building. "This is it."

He stared, unmoving.

"Robert." She held out her hand. "I need my bags."

"Tell me one thing," he said. "Why did you do it?"

Jenny glanced at her watch and blew out an exasperated breath. "Do what?"

"Wait so long to get your belly button pierced."

It didn't take a genius to know he didn't really care about the answer. For whatever reason, he just wasn't ready to say good-bye. Normally she wouldn't mind lingering. But right now she didn't have time for games.

"I always wanted to do it," Jenny said hurriedly.

"But my father has this thing against piercing and his approval always meant a lot to me."

"That surprises me," Robert said. "I'd never peg you as the type to care what your dad—or anyone—thinks."

"Get real," Jenny said with a laugh, taking her bags from his hand. "We all want our parents' approval. Their opinions matter . . . no matter what we try to tell ourselves."

Seven

"Why do you want to leave Dodson and Dodson?" Lloyd Carman's brows pulled together. "It's one of the largest CPA firms in Chicago. They have great benefits."

Annie looked up from her piece of birthday cake, a tiny pout touching her lips. "Why are we talking about *her*? This is *my* birthday."

All Jenny had wanted to do after her job interview was take some ibuprofen and veg out at home. She certainly hadn't wanted to go out to eat with the family for her sister's birthday. But these types of events were sacred in the Carman household, and no excuse was good enough. So, Jenny had taken a couple of Advil and gotten to the restaurant early.

"Let Jenny finish telling her story, Lloyd," Carol said to her husband. She shifted her gaze to Annie. "It may be your birthday but that

doesn't mean the evening has to completely re-
volve around you."

Jenny forked a bite of cake but didn't raise it
to her mouth. "I only interviewed for the job. It
went extremely well and they appeared interested. But they're not going to be extending any
offers for at least a month."

"Kyllie's is cool," Annie said. "Did you wear
what you have on to the interview?"

"I hope you wore a suit," her father said before she could answer. "You can never go wrong
wearing a suit."

"I wasn't sure if I was too casual," Jenny said,
ignoring her dad's comment. "But the woman
who interviewed me seemed okay with it. In
fact she even complimented me."

While it sounded crazy, Jenny had the feeling her stylish attire had weighed as heavily in
her favor as her accounting résumé.

"You look good," Annie said grudgingly. "I
love your hair."

Jenny raised a hand to her head. "I look in
the mirror and don't even recognize myself."

"Be glad," Annie said in a deep voice more
suited to a Halloween movie. "Be very, very
glad."

"Annie," Carol said sharply.

Jenny just laughed. "It's okay, Mom. Annie's right. I did look like a frump."

"Just don't go changing too much," her father said. "We love you just the way you are."

A warmth rose up inside Jenny, and she realized how true the words were that she'd spoken to Robert earlier. Having her father's approval was important. Unfortunately, she already knew he wasn't going to like what she had to say next.

But there was no time like the present to break the news. After all, when she stood up to leave the restaurant, they'd find out anyway.

"Before I went to my interview I did something I've been wanting to do for a long time," Jenny said.

"You bought a condo?" Her father leaned forward, his hands gripping the table's edge. "Without even letting me check it first?"

Jenny had been looking at places for the past year but had been waiting to get serious until after her promotion. She could only hope her dad would be so relieved she hadn't bought a house that he wouldn't care about the belly button ring.

"No," she said. "No new condo. But I do have a new belly button ring."

"A what?" Lloyd's voice rose and cracked.

Her mother laid a calming hand on his arm.

"Cool." Annie shifted her gaze to her mother. "Can I get mine done, too? Please?"

"Absolutely not," her father snapped. He might have spoken to his younger daughter, but his gaze never left Jenny. "What in the name of all that's holy were you thinking?"

It was as close as her father ever came to swearing. But it was his reddened face and tightly pressed together lips that told her he was ready to blow.

At one time Jenny might have sunk back against the booth, but spunky Jasmine would never tolerate cowering.

"I wanted one and I'm an adult." Jenny lifted her chin and met her father's gaze head on. "The way I look at it, it's my body. If I choose to have a little ring in my belly button, that's my business."

Jenny felt stronger and more like an adult with each word.

"You go girl," Annie said.

"You're not planning to have any more piercing done, are you?" her mother asked in a worried tone.

"Not at this point," Jenny said.

Her father's face turned ashen. "Dear God, where did I go wrong?"

"Dad," Jenny said patiently. "It's just a belly button ring."

"You used to be so sensible. Now you're putting stripes in your hair, rings in your body, and doing goodness knows what else." Her father raked his fingers through his thinning hair. When he shifted his gaze to Jenny, his expression was more puzzled than angry. "What's happening to you?"

"I guess I'm growing up, Dad," Jenny said. "I'm finally growing up."

"You're going to cut his hair?" Marcee let out a whoop of laughter that resounded across the phone line. "Have you forgotten what happened when you trimmed your sister's bangs?"

Jenny's fingers tightened around the receiver. On her way home from the restaurant, Robert had called. The second he'd clicked off, she'd speed dialed Marcee.

"When he asked for an appointment, I was so surprised I didn't know what to say," Jenny said. "I tried to put him off but he wouldn't take no for an answer."

Though a hint of exasperation filled her tone, secretly Jenny was pleased by his refusal to wait.

"You know this isn't about a haircut, don't you?"

"What other reason could there be?"

"He wants you." Marcee moaned the words and Jenny couldn't help but smile. "He wants you back in his bed. And he wants *you* bad."

Excitement skittered up Jenny's spine, but she refused to get her hopes up. "Like I told you the other day, he's working on a merger and doesn't have time—"

"And like I told you," Marcee interrupted, "men always have time for a little nookie."

Jenny had to admit that just hearing Robert's deep voice had been enough to cause a shiver of desire to skitter up her spine. She'd found herself wishing that his call *had* been about having her back in his bed rather than his hair.

"That's all well and good," Jenny said. "But he's stopping by Kristy's salon late tomorrow afternoon expecting me to have my scissors ready."

The other end of the phone line grew strangely quiet. "I guess then you have two options."

"And what would those be?"

"You're either going to have to learn to cut hair," Marcee said, "or seduce him in the back room. Knowing your experience with scissors, I'd say go for the seduction."

* * *

Jenny eyed the fake head of hair sitting on the counter in front of her, feeling jittery and more than a little scared. She wanted to see Robert. She was excited he'd called. She just didn't want to cut his hair.

She glanced out one of the floor-to-ceiling windows at the front of Kristy Theiler's salon. If only she were out there now enjoying the warm spring day, instead of standing at Kristy's workstation, feeling like a fish out of water, becoming more frustrated with each snip of the shears.

"Hold the scissors more at an angle." Kristy blew out a harsh breath, telling Jenny she wasn't the only one frustrated. "Like this."

For what had to be the hundredth time since Jenny had entered the trendy Highland Park salon, her friend and hairstylist extraordinaire demonstrated the proper technique for trimming hair.

Kristy shoved the scissors back in Jenny's hand, giving her no choice but to take them again. And to try . . . again. Positioning them at an angle, Jenny held her breath and snipped. A hunk of hair from the wig perched on a Styrofoam head in front of her dropped to the shiny hardwood floor.

Jenny stared at the now lopsided hairpiece

and chewed on her lip. "This is a lot harder than it looks."

Kristy cringed but somehow still managed a smile. "We all have special talents," she said in a reassuring tone. "Cutting hair just doesn't seem to be one of yours."

"Manual dexterity has never come easily for me," Jenny admitted.

Except with Robert, she thought wistfully, when she'd surprised herself—and him—with what she could do with her hands.

"I still don't understand why you told this guy your name was Jasmine and that you owned a hair salon." Puzzlement filled Kristy's large blue eyes.

Jenny could understand her friend's confusion. As far as Kristy knew, Robert was just a guy she'd met when she was out with friends and feeling silly. In the *Reader's Digest* condensed version she'd given her friend, all they'd done was talk.

Discretion was the name of the game. While Kristy would be the first to admit she'd been tempted when she and her husband had dated, Kristy had been a virgin when she'd married. Unlike Marcee, Kristy would be appalled at the notion of a one-night stand.

"I was just trying to add a little fun to the conversation. Fun name," Jenny said. "Fun job."

The only other employee still in the shop choked back a laugh. "There's nothing fun about standing on your feet for eight hours or trying to please women who look like Rosie O'Donnell but want to be transformed into J-Lo."

Jenny smiled in understanding. "That's my point. We all want to be someone else. I know it isn't good to lie but since I didn't plan to see him again, I figured what would it hurt?"

Kristy's dimples flashed. "Before Ray and I were married, I went on a cruise and gave myself a whole new identity."

The other stylist nodded. "When I was in high school, my friend and I used to go to parties at DePaul and pretend we were college girls."

"I hope I don't live to regret it," Jenny said, catching sight of Robert's Land Rover pulling into a stall in front of the shop.

"Making up a new identity?" Kristy asked.

"No." The blood ran cold in Jenny's veins, and she shivered. "Cutting his hair."

"Is that him?" Kristy asked, peering over Jenny's shoulder.

Jenny nodded and took a deep, steadying breath. "Looks like it's showtime."

She dropped the scissors and moved to the front counter. Kristy quickly followed.

As much as she didn't want to cut his hair, Jenny was eager to see Robert again. A quiver of excitement traveled up her spine, and it took all her resolve not to look up when the bells over the door jingled. But she kept her gaze focused on Kristy and pretended to be deeply engrossed in conversation.

"You look great, by the way," Kristy said in a low tone.

Kristy was notoriously stingy with compliments, and the knowledge that she looked good bolstered Jenny's confidence. While Kristy and the other stylist looked perfectly presentable in black pants and crisp white shirts, Jenny had chosen to wear a dress.

The way the red fabric clung to her curves made her feel sexy and desirable. And she hoped the low neckline would draw Robert's attention from her lack of skill with the scissors.

Kristy continued to talk but she might as well have been speaking Chinese. The moment Robert had walked through the door, she'd sensed his presence and her body had started to hum with anticipation.

"Jasmine."

Jenny looked up. She widened her eyes. "Robert. I didn't hear the door."

His lips lifted in an easy smile and her heart skipped a beat. "Thanks for fitting me in."

The moment his gaze locked with hers, the funky music and salon conversation faded away. The pull she felt toward him was stronger than any magnet. Raw, physical . . . emotional.

"My pleasure." Jenny's voice came out low and husky with a sensual edge.

"Aren't you going to introduce me?" Kristy asked.

Jenny jerked her attention to her friend, and the connection between her and Robert shattered.

"Of course," she said, suddenly mindful of Kristy's curious gaze. "Robert Marshall, this is my friend and coworker Kristy Theiler. Kristy is in charge of the shop whenever . . . well, whenever I'm not here."

Robert's gaze shifted to Kristy. He extended his hand. "Nice to meet you."

Kristy let her gaze linger on his handsome face. "You sure don't look like you need a haircut to me."

Jenny shot Kristy a warning glance before offering Robert a broad smile. "I'll show you my station."

Robert followed her across the tiled floor, and she added a little sway to her hips. She'd dabbed on a liberal dose of perfume and hoped the sultry scent followed in her wake.

It was the same fragrance she'd worn the night they spent together. The same fragrance that she hoped still lingered on his pillow. The same fragrance that now caused an ache of longing to fill her body every time she applied it to her pulse points.

She stopped beside a chair at the far end of the salon. "Here we are."

He moved past her to take a seat in the black leather chair, and somehow his arm brushed against her breast. Another woman might have moved back or chided him for being careless.

Jenny did neither. She merely looked at him through lowered lids as a thousand frantic butterflies beat their wings against the wall of her stomach.

Just standing close enough to touch and kiss him made her blood run hot and her body ache. His eyes were dark and teasing and . . . tempting. Challenging her to be Jasmine.

Jasmine, who'd seen what she wanted and gone after it.

Jasmine, who'd done things Jenny had only read about.

Jasmine, who'd embraced her sensuality and made a night with this man a night to remember.

One glance from his blue eyes turned the blood in her veins from room temperature to fiery hot. And when his gaze locked on hers, she sank in a quicksand of desire. Judging from the heat in his eyes, he felt it, too.

"Nice."

Jenny assumed he was talking about Kristy's stylish workstation, but Jasmine wasn't so naïve. She realized that the thoughts behind those gorgeous eyes had nothing to do with beveled mirrors and marble countertops.

The familiar shyness surfaced, and for a second Jenny didn't know what to say, much less what to do about the desire coursing through her body.

What would Jasmine do?

She'd go after what she wanted.

Jenny let her gaze travel the length of his body, lingering for a second just below his midsection. And when her gaze lifted and met his, she leaned close, resting her arm across the back of the chair.

"You look nice in that suit." She dropped her voice to a low tone and paused for effect. "But I think I like you better naked."

Heat flared again in his eyes, and Jenny felt a surge of triumph. She straightened, but he grabbed her hand, pulling her closer to him.

The mere touch of his skin against hers turned her knees to jelly.

"Think?" His teasing tone made her smile. "You don't know? After all, you've seen me both ways. Unless you've forgotten and need a reminder?"

"Maybe I do need a reminder." Her lips curved upward. "But this is a little too public. Want to check out the back room?"

Eight

Robert's eyes widened, and Jenny could tell she'd caught him off-guard with her boldness. The knowledge pleased her and gave her the confidence to take the challenge a step further.

She leaned close and raked her fingers through his hair. "You don't need a haircut," she said in a professional tone, smoothing the hair she'd just ruffled. "Besides, we both know that's not why you're here."

The words came out seductively soft, and his lips curved upward.

"I haven't been able to stop thinking about you," he admitted in a husky voice.

Satisfaction flowed through Jenny's veins like warm honey, but she merely shrugged. "I've thought about you once or twice, too."

He suddenly leaned close. "Liar."

Jenny's mouth went dry. "What did you say?"

"I've crossed your mind *at least* three or four times," he teased. "Don't try to tell me otherwise."

Jenny exhaled the breath she'd been holding.

"Okay." She heaved an exaggerated sigh. "Three. But I'm sure that's all it was."

"And I'll bet you've thought of even more fantasies that I could fulfill." His eyes glittered with an intensity belied by the lighthearted words.

"I may have had a fleeting thought or two," she admitted.

"Because I did such a good job on Friday," he said with typical male humility.

"Good?" Jenny shook her head. "That wouldn't be the word I'd use."

Robert's smile stilled. "Okay, I may have been a little rusty. But—"

"Silly man." He looked so serious, Jenny couldn't help but laugh. "You were *fabulous*."

His smile returned, nearly blinding her with its dazzle. "That's why you want me naked in the back room."

Robert, Jenny decided, must have forgotten where they were or he'd have never spoken so loud. She glanced around the salon, hoping no one had overheard. Thankfully, Kristy was on the phone at the front desk, while the other stylist was busy blow-drying a client's hair.

"Shhh." Jenny pressed her finger against his lips. "That's our little secret."

"It's no secret that I love the way you taste." He captured her hand and brought it to his mouth, nibbling on her fingers. "Spicy but with a hint of sugar."

She hadn't forgotten the taste of him, either. Or the feel of him. Or his touch. Desire, hot and insistent, shot through Jenny.

"Would you do it?" she asked, her voice breathless. "Would you get naked for me?"

Though Jenny had kept her voice discreetly low, she once again glanced around the shop. The remaining stylist had just finished with her customer, while Kristy appeared to be closing out the cash register.

"Right now?" Robert asked, pulling her attention back to him. "Right here?"

"An audience could be fun." Jenny batted her lashes. "Give the customers something to talk about."

"I'm up for it." Robert loosened his tie, his eyes dark and intense. "Say the word."

Jenny paused, excitement skittering up her spine. How far would he take the game?

"Okay," she said. "I'll say the word."

Jenny leaned close. Her breath fluttered against his ear.

"Later," she whispered.

Just like the other night, Robert didn't disappoint. He chuckled, slid an arm around her waist, and pulled her close. "Promise?"

Jenny batted her three-coats-of-mascara lashes. "What do you think?"

"I think I like you," he said. Her heart skipped a beat.

"You just want to see *me* naked," she said.

He grinned. "That, too."

For several heartbeats neither of them spoke.

"What's up?" Kristy's question came out more demanding than curious, her voice sounding unnaturally shrill in the silence.

Robert glanced at Kristy but didn't answer, apparently deciding it was up to Jenny to respond to her "employee."

Jenny shot Robert a wink and turned to face her friend. "What does it look like? I'm doing a consultation."

Kristy opened her mouth to speak but Jenny wasn't taking any chances. When Kristy got flustered, you never knew what she might say.

"My professional opinion"—Jenny paused for effect—"is that Robert doesn't need a haircut. In fact, it might look a little funky if I cut it now."

"Smart call." Relief skittered across Kristy's face. The blond smiled at Robert. "Your hair looks good. You really are better off not letting her touch it."

Jenny felt Robert's curious gaze and sensed he wasn't sure what to make of Kristy's odd comment.

"Better off not letting her touch it?" Jenny put her hands on her hips and forced a note of wry humor into her voice. "Gee thanks, Kristy. Your confidence in me is inspiring."

Robert reached over and gave Jenny's shoulder a reassuring squeeze. "I'm not afraid to have you cut my hair."

Jenny bit her lip to keep from smiling. The sentiment was sweet, but oh so misplaced. If only the man knew how close he'd come to looking like a refugee from a prison gang . . .

Kristy covered her mouth with her hand, and Jenny knew her friend was trying not to laugh.

"I'm leaving," the other stylist called out, her hand on the front door. "Good night everyone."

Kristy glanced at her watch. Her eyes widened. "I didn't realize it was so late. I need to get going, too."

"I can lock up," Jenny offered.

Kristy hesitated only a second. "Sure you don't mind?"

"Not at all."

Kristy reached into her pocket and pulled out a key. "Just bring it back next time you're in."

Jenny's fingers closed around the key, and Kristy hurried out the front door.

Robert's brows pulled together in puzzlement. "Why did your employee give you a key to your own shop?"

"I forgot mine today." Jenny lifted her lips in a self-deprecating smile. She continued without missing a beat. "I realized I didn't have the key the minute I pulled into the parking lot, but didn't feel like going back for it."

Robert nodded, appearing to accept the explanation.

"I can always count on Kristy," Jenny continued. "She's super organized. In fact, I bet she could run this place better than I."

Robert shook his head. "I don't believe that."

The warm blue of his eyes made her pulse stutter. There was just something about this man, something about his nearness, his touch, his confidence in her that made her go all soft and mushy inside.

But men didn't like mushy. Men liked bold. Men liked Jasmine.

Jenny gazed at him through lowered lashes. "Want a tour of the place before I close up?"

A spark flickered in the back of his eyes. "Would this *tour* include the back room?"

"Of course." Jenny held out her hand to him.

The hand that closed over hers was warm and the look in his eyes full of promise. Her knees began to tremble. Still, she somehow managed to make it to the door. Pulling it open, she flicked on the light. The room was more serviceable than stylish, with shelves full of hair care products and an area that served as an employee break room.

Robert stepped inside and pulled the door shut behind him. It was then that Jenny realized that for the first time since she'd left his condo, they were alone. The room, as large as any executive's office, shrank to cubicle size.

Her heart fluttered in her chest.

Jenny let her gaze sweep over him, taking in the lean hips, muscular chest, and broad shoulders. She'd explored every inch of that body last week, but, in retrospect, far too quickly. There was so much more she could do if she had the time . . .

"Jasmine?"

She met his gaze, excitement coursing up her spine. "Take off your clothes."

His eyes widened. "Why?"

"I need a reminder," she said. "I need to see if you look better naked or in a suit."

Robert glanced around the room. "You really want to do this here?"

His hesitation took her by surprise. "Yeah."

"I've never been naked in a place of business before," he said.

"There's a first time for everything." Jenny reached up and loosened his tie. "The employees and customers are gone. Right now, it's just you and me."

She wasn't sure if it was the words or her touch that convinced him, but when heat flared in his eyes, she knew she had him. His gaze flickered over the red clingy fabric of her dress. "Will you be getting naked, too?"

"Eventually." She shot him an impudent smile and put her hands on her hips. "But enough talk. It's time to remind Judge Jasmine what you've got."

Robert didn't move a muscle. Instead he crossed his arms and leaned against a cabinet. "First some ground rules."

He looked so serious that Jenny's heart skipped a beat. "Such as?"

"No video recordings or flash photography." His face was expressionless. Only a twitch in a corner of his lips gave him away.

The tension that had gripped her shoulders eased. He was merely getting into the game, seizing back some of the control she'd taken. "Any other demands?"

"Every time I take something off, I get a kiss." His innocent expression was at odds with the devilish sparkle in his eyes.

While she liked the concept, Jenny didn't want to appear too eager. "And once your clothes are off?"

"You decide if I should put them back on." He paused for an extra heartbeat. "Or if we should make the most of the situation."

His boyish smile was nearly her undoing. If she didn't get a grip on herself, *she* was going to be the one doing the stripping.

"I agree to the terms," she said in her best "Judge Jasmine" tone. "But I warn you, I'm an expert at making the most of any situation."

"I'm counting on it." Robert grinned. His fingers moved to his throat, and with a single fluid gesture he removed the silk tie and sent it flying across the room.

He shot Jenny an expectant look.

She circled him, then rose on her tiptoes and brushed his ear with her lips.

"What was that?"

"You didn't specify where I had to kiss you." She lowered her voice to a sultry whisper. "That's really to your advantage. Think of all the possibilities . . . once you're naked."

He looked down at his belt, then lifted his gaze to meet hers. A light of understanding filled his eyes.

A tingle began deep in her belly.

Impulsively she placed her hands on his shoulders and lifted her face to his. His mouth was warm and sweet. Though Jenny wanted to linger, she dropped her hands and took a step back.

"That still wasn't much of a kiss," he said.

"A tie's not much clothing," she shot back.

"So taking off the socks next might not be a smart move?"

Jenny lifted a shoulder in a shrug, pretending not to see the twinkle in his eyes. "Totally up to you."

He studied her thoughtfully for a moment. His fingers dropped to his belt, and he fiddled with the buckle.

She held her breath.

Finally, just when she thought she couldn't

stand the suspense another second, Robert removed his suit coat and draped it across a chair.

Then, without missing a beat, he grabbed her hand and pulled her tight against him. His lips closed over hers, hard and demanding.

Electricity raced from Jenny's lips all the way to her toes. She raised her arms and slid her fingers through his hair, savoring the feel of his body against hers, drinking in the taste of him.

But when his tongue swept her lips seeking entry, she steeled her resolve and turned her mouth from his.

"There's no skin showing." Her breath came in fast, short puffs, and her heart pounded a bongo rhythm in her chest.

"Easily remedied." A tiny dimple flashed in his cheek.

Robert unbuttoned the cuffs of his shirt before moving to his shirtfront. His fingers nimbly moved from one button to another. The crisp white shirt was off before Jenny's heart had a chance to return to a normal rhythm.

Some men let themselves go when they passed thirty, but not Robert. As if compelled, Jenny's gaze moved down his body, lingering on the muscles of his chest. She swallowed hard against the lump in her throat.

He was just as beautiful as she remembered.

"Come here." Soft and low, his voice held an enticing undercurrent.

She forced herself to stay still. To take another look. To slow things down and savor the moment. To make him wait. So that he'd remember the passion . . . and her.

But she hadn't considered her own desire. With her own need pushing her forward, Jenny closed the distance between them more quickly than she'd intended. Once she reached him the air crackled and sparked. Taking her time no longer held any appeal.

Still, she started out slow, pressing her lips softly against his.

On a low groan, Robert pulled her hard against him. Heartbeat met heartbeat. Need met need. She melted deeper into the kiss and whimpered in protest when his lips left her mouth to scatter kisses down her neck.

Delightful shivers shot through her stomach, shifting lower and . . . lower still.

"You are so beautiful." He placed his open mouth on her neck, nipping and suckling until he found a sensitive spot that made her gasp. The wanting turned to an ache.

By the time his mouth returned to hers, Jenny desperately wanted everything he could give and she wanted it *now*.

When he urged her to open her mouth, she welcomed the penetrating slide of his tongue with unrestrained enthusiasm. He stroked long and slow, hot and deep, and she kissed him back the same way, pressing her body against his.

Jenny could feel his erection, hard and stiff at the crux of her thighs. A fiery heat engulfed her, and the knowledge that he wanted her as much as she wanted him made her bold.

She pointed to his trousers. "Those have to go."

Without a word he unbuckled his belt, slid open the button at his waistband, and pulled down the zipper. The pants dropped to pool at his feet. Without shifting his gaze from her, he stepped out of the trousers and nudged them to the side with his foot.

Jenny shivered and let the essence of him wash over her, breathing in the scent of soap, shaving cream, and masculine desire. He was just as she'd remembered. Sculpted pecs. Taut abdomen. Enormous erection that the paisley boxers couldn't begin to conceal.

"I've got an idea where you could kiss me next," he said when her gaze lingered.

"Great minds think alike," she murmured.

She flattened her palms against his bare chest, caressing his taut, heated flesh, and strummed her fingers down to his waist. His erection pulsed against the boxers, and without hesitating she slid her hand inside the paisley silk.

Robert took a quick breath but made no move to stop her. Not even when her hand settled around his rock-hard shaft.

Jenny stroked the silky skin with her palm, her fingers circling the ridge, measuring his length with a slow, sliding stroke.

The rigid shaft bucked and pulsated. Still, she stroked.

"Jasmine." The word burst from his lips like a strangled moan.

Satisfaction surged through her. Jenny might have hesitated, but Jasmine didn't think twice. She sank to her knees. Her tongue swirled gently over the velvety flesh.

"You don't have to—" he protested weakly.

Jenny lifted her head for a moment and smiled. "I *want* to."

Before he could say anything further, she lowered her head and began to lick him with deliberate swipes of her tongue. Then she closed her lips over the tip of his penis and began to suck gently.

"Ohmigod, Jasmine." He cupped the back of her head in his palm, and his breathing grew fast and shallow. The muscles in his abdomen flexed and rippled.

Sensing he was only moments away from release, Jenny paused and took all of him in one swooping motion.

Ting, ting, ting.

The sound of the bells over the front door ricocheted through her head, penetrating the fog of desire clouding her brain with the realization that they were no longer alone.

Her head jerked up and she caught the edge of Robert's shaft with her top teeth.

With an explicit curse, he took a step back.

"What's the matter?" he asked, his voice raw and hoarse.

"Shhh." Jenny scrambled to her feet, her heart racing. "Someone's here."

"Are you sure?"

Jenny nodded, glad he'd followed her example and kept his voice low.

"Cleaning crew?" he asked.

Considering the fact that the cleaning supplies were stored in the room where they stood, Jenny could only hope that wasn't the case.

"I don't know." Clasping her hands together to still their trembling, Jenny forced a bright smile and confident demeanor. "I'll stall. You get dressed."

"I don't want you to go out there alone." He reached for his pants.

"I'll be fine." Taking a deep breath, Jenny straightened her dress and stepped out of the room, pulling the door closed behind her. Her gaze swept the salon.

Up at the front desk, a blond head was bent over, rummaging behind the counter.

Jenny recognized the spiky tufts of hair immediately.

"Kristy." Thankfully, even to Jenny's own ears, her voice sounded surprisingly steady. "What are you looking for?"

"My parents' anniversary is tonight." Kristy straightened and held up a small oblong box wrapped in shiny purple paper. "I forgot the gift."

Her gaze slipped over Jenny's shoulder, and Jenny knew she was looking for Robert.

"Then it's good you came back," Jenny spoke quickly, not wanting to give her friend the opportunity to ask any questions. "I mean you can't go to a party without a gift. Although I'm sure your parents really don't care about presents. They have so much . . ."

Jenny realized she was babbling but she wasn't about to stop now. Not when there was so much at stake. Being caught in flagrante delicto by a janitor was one thing. But if her friend walked in and found Robert putting on his pants . . .

"Where's Ray?" Jenny asked when she ran out of air.

"In the car."

Jenny opened her mouth again but Kristy was faster. "Where's Robert?"

Jenny wished she could say he'd already left, but the fact that she could still see his Land Rover through the salon's front window shot down that option.

"Robert?" Jenny asked, trying to buy him a few more seconds.

Kristy rolled her eyes. "Mr. I'm-so-lucky-she-didn't-cut-my-hair guy?"

"Oh, him." Jenny gestured in the general direction of the storage room. "In the back."

She couldn't think of a reason for him to be there so she didn't elaborate.

Kristy's gaze narrowed, and Jenny knew her eagle-eyed friend missed nothing. Not her disheveled hair. Not her fiery hot cheeks. And especially not the love bite Robert had planted on her neck.

Years ago her father had caught her and the minister's son kissing on the front porch. Jenny had fallen all over herself trying to explain that it wasn't what it looked like. She'd only made things worse.

But Jenny wasn't sixteen. And she didn't have to answer for her behavior. She kept her mouth shut and turned her attention to the brushes and combs at the nearby workstation.

"He seems nice," Kristy said finally.

Jenny glanced into the mirror, and Kristy's concerned face reflected back at her. "Robert's a good friend."

"Friend?" Kristy's mouth twisted in a wry smile. "I saw how he looked at you."

"Next time I'm letting it go to voice mail."

Jenny jumped at the sound of Robert's deep voice. She turned and exhaled the breath she'd been holding. Not only was he fully clothed, he looked like he'd just stepped out of a boardroom. Not a hair—or button—was out of place.

"The call wasn't important?" Jenny wasn't sure where he was going with this, but she was willing to play along.

At Kristy's curious look, Robert smiled ruefully. "It could easily have waited."

The fact that he didn't go on and on about the fictitious call made it all the more believable.

His gaze shifted to Jenny briefly before returning to Kristy. "Jasmine and I thought we'd grab some dinner. Would you like to join us?"

It was the first Jenny had heard about the plans, but she was up for some food. She slanted a sideways glance at Robert and her lips quirked upward. Assuming, of course, that he could be the dessert.

"I'd love to." Regret filled Kristy's gaze. "But it's my parents' anniversary and we're on our way to Des Plaines."

"What time do you need to be there?" Jenny asked.

Kristy glanced down at her watch and yelped. "Five minutes ago."

In the doorway, the blond stopped and turned. "But I'd love to take a raincheck—"

The sound of a horn honking interrupted her words.

"You'd better hurry," Jenny said.

She breathed a sigh of relief when Kristy wiggled her fingers good-bye and slipped out the door.

"You're so good." Jenny turned back to Robert. "That bit about the phone call was inspired."

"You're the one who's good." His gaze lingered on her mouth. "At everything."

Nine

She wasn't *really* good at everything, Jenny decided. Certainly not at picking restaurants. She gazed at Robert over the tabletop. When he'd asked her to pick the place after their aborted "game" of sexual give-and-take, her normally razor-sharp mind had frozen.

The only restaurant she'd been able to think of was Nookies, a popular diner in Lincoln Park. While the food was fabulous and the prices reasonable, the atmosphere could hardly be considered romantic.

Robert was being a good sport, but she'd seen the look of surprise on his face when he'd walked in and seen the tabletops covered in Formica and the serviceable linoleum that had clearly seen better days. Thankfully, though the place was crowded, they didn't have to wait.

In a matter of minutes, they were given a table in a front window alcove.

The waiter appeared almost immediately, and it wasn't long until their order was taken and their drinks on the table in front of them.

"The food is really good here." Jenny forced enthusiasm into her voice. She'd botched it again. A hip and cool woman would never have chosen this place for an intimate dinner.

"Judging by the crowd," Robert said, scanning the restaurant's interior, "I'd say that's a given."

His gaze swept right past a gorgeous woman with thick chestnut hair and ivory skin, standing at the cash register. But the woman wasn't so quick to dismiss him. She blatantly stared at Jenny's companion, her big green eyes sparkling with undisguised interest.

Jenny was intimidated.

Jasmine was irritated.

While one night of passion might not make Robert hers, he was with her now. With Jasmine egging her on, Jenny shot the woman a back-off-he's-mine warning glance.

The redhead lifted her chin and shifted her gaze.

Satisfied, Jenny turned her attention back to Robert. "Lots of people come here for the chocolate chip pancakes."

He raised a brow.

"Topped with whipped cream," she added.

"Whipped cream," Robert mused. "It's good on almost anything."

His voice was low and smooth as silk. Jenny tingled all the way to the tips of her toes as she imagined his hands spreading the creamy substance all over her body . . . then slowly licking it off. Or better yet, her hands spreading it over *him* . . .

Her tongue moistened her lips.

His eyes darkened. "It's a perfect night for whipped cream."

A curious thrumming filled her body.

"But I didn't order pancakes." She kept her gaze fixed on him. "Remember?"

"Can I get you a refill?" The gangly waiter stood beside the table, a pitcher of iced tea in one hand. "Or anything else right now?"

Robert blinked. "I'm fine."

"Me, too," Jenny added.

The interruption only lasted a second, but when Robert met her gaze again, the fire in his eyes was gone and his smile was merely polite.

"You should have told him you wanted the pancakes," he said. "Instead of the soup."

Jenny frowned, wondering if she'd misread his signals. It was possible. She'd never been intuitive. Perhaps she'd been thinking whipped-cream-on-the-body while he'd been thinking whipped-cream-on-the-pancakes. It was a depressing realization.

"If I'd wanted *pancakes*"—disappointment made her tone sharp—"I'd have ordered them."

The words came out blunt but Robert just laughed.

"You're not one to mince words." Approval laced his deep, sexy voice. "My sister-in-law, Stacy, is a lot like you."

Jenny looked up and discovered the warmth had returned to his eyes. A faint flutter of hope rose inside her. Perhaps he *was* still interested. It was clear he held his sister-in-law in high regard.

"I didn't know you have a brother."

She'd wondered about his family. There had been no pictures in his condo. And while they'd discussed her family that first night, they'd never gotten around to his.

We were too busy with other things.

Her heart skipped a beat. "What's his name?"

"William," Robert said. "Everyone calls him Will."

"Sort of like everyone calls you Rob."

A puzzled look crossed his face. "No they don't."

"I did." Before she could stop herself, she

slanted him a flirtatious glance and asked seductively, "When we were in bed? Remember?"

He chuckled, a low, pleasant, rumbling sound. "I must have been too caught up in what was going on to notice."

"Are you saying I swept you off your feet?"

His smile broadened. "It would seem so."

Try as she might, Jenny couldn't remember a single instance when *she'd* swept anyone off his feet. But things had changed. She'd changed. Feeling oddly triumphant, Jenny leaned back in her seat, suddenly more optimistic about the evening's outcome.

"Is your brother older or younger?" she asked.

"Younger," Robert said. "He just turned thirty."

"And he already has a wife." Jenny couldn't imagine how she'd feel if her little sister made it to the altar before her.

"He's been married since he got out of college," Robert said. "He even has a child."

"He's my age," Jenny said, almost to herself. "And he already has a family."

A weight settled across her chest. She shouldn't be surprised. It seemed like all her friends were married and had children. Except Marcee, of course. "What does he do for a living?"

A tiny muscle jumped in Robert's jaw. "He runs the family business."

"Sounds like you're both successful." Jenny sensed an undercurrent of tension in the air, but couldn't figure out why. "Any other kids in your family?"

"Just the two of us." He took a sip of tea and tilted his head. "How about you?"

"One sister. Annie." Jenny couldn't help but sigh. "She's seventeen."

"Do you see her much?"

Jenny started to say every Sunday, until she remembered the story she'd concocted that first night.

"Arizona is too far away," Jenny said. "But even if she and I lived in the same house, I doubt we'd spend much time together."

Way back when, they'd been close. Annie's first word had been *Jen*. When Jenny had left for college, her little sister had cried for days. But that bond seemed a lifetime ago.

Robert smiled encouragingly.

"We're so different," she said. "I'd like to be Annie's friend, but I feel like I hardly know her."

The truth twisted in her chest, bringing a profound sadness.

"My brother and I used to be close." Robert's

gaze took on a faraway look. "But several years ago that changed."

Though his tone was offhand, the sadness in his eyes said this was no casual matter. "What happened?"

Robert shifted in his seat. His lips pressed together.

Jenny couldn't believe she'd been so forward. What had happened between him and his brother was not her business. And, unlike her snoopy little sister, Jenny had always gone out of her way *not* to pry.

"He took something that belonged to me," Robert said finally.

Jenny gasped. "He stole from you?"

Robert opened his mouth but closed it when the waiter appeared with their food. He waited until the man left before he spoke.

"Not in the strict sense of the word." His inscrutable look gave nothing away. "Let's just say he knew it should have been mine, but it fell into his lap and he took it without saying a word."

Jenny was more confused than ever. But she was done asking questions. He'd had the opportunity to explain and he'd chosen not to elaborate.

Besides, she'd seen the hurt behind the indifference. And she, more than most, understood the heartbreak of a sibling relationship gone bad.

Impulsively she reached across the table and squeezed his hand.

"When my sister started high school, she told her friends she was an only child." Jenny forced a laugh, though she still didn't find it funny.

Robert's brows pulled together. "Why would she do that?"

"Annie is cool," Jenny said, trying to keep her tone offhand. "Pretty. Stylish. Popular with boys. I didn't meet her standards."

For a second a bewildered look filled his gaze. "I don't understand that. Not at all."

Jenny shrugged. Her mother might say it was typical teen stuff, but for Jenny the incident clearly illustrated how far apart she and Annie had grown. How she wished things could be different . . .

Tears sprang to her eyes but she quickly blinked them back before Robert could see.

"I know that must have hurt." His hand closed over hers. "How is it now between you and your sister?"

Jenny thought for a moment. "I'm still not cool enough for her."

"How could anyone think you're not cool?"

The shock in his voice warmed her heart. "You're the most beautiful, together woman I've ever met."

"That's what you probably say to all the girls you want to sleep with," Jenny retorted, but softened the words with a teasing smile.

The waiter returned with more iced tea and Jenny changed the subject. While they ate she made a determined effort to keep the conversation light and Jasmine-like. The result was that time flew by and a smile rarely left Robert's face.

"I'm in the mood for ice cream," Jenny said after the waiter left to get their check.

"Not whipped cream?" he teased.

She leaned across the table and motioned him forward.

"Ice cream now," she whispered in his ear. "Whipped cream later."

"Don't make promises you don't intend to keep."

She met his gaze. "I'm not."

Robert smiled. "I'll get the waiter."

He started to raise his hand but Jenny stopped him. "I was thinking more along the lines of the Baskin-Robbins on Halsted. We could walk?"

"Sounds good to me."

Robert picked up the check and dropped a generous tip on the table before they headed out the door.

The sun had set and the temperature had dropped a good ten degrees since they'd entered the restaurant. Jenny quickly discovered that the thin fabric of her dress provided little protection from the brisk breeze.

But she refused to complain. After all, walking *had* been her idea. Still, after only three blocks she couldn't keep from shivering.

"You're cold." Robert stopped in the middle of the sidewalk, paying no attention to the people forced to sidestep around them.

"Just a little." Jenny pressed her lips together to keep her teeth from chattering. "But we're almost there."

Concern deepened the blue hue of his eyes. Without saying a word, he took off his suit jacket.

"You don't have to—" she protested.

"I want to," he said firmly, draping it across her shoulders.

The chivalrous gesture warmed her to the tips of her toes. She snuggled in the jacket, breathing in his cologne. It was a subtle scent with a slightly citrus twang, and it conjured up all sorts of memories of the last time she smelled it, the last time she'd tasted it on his skin.

"Here we are."

Lost in thought, Jenny glanced up, surprised to find Robert reaching for the door handle of the brightly lit ice cream store.

She gestured for him to go inside, but Robert shook his head.

"How about tonight you let me be a gentleman?" he said with a wink.

She smiled, feeling lighthearted. "As long as I don't have to be a lady."

They ordered two chocolate chip cones and sat down at one of the small tables.

"Chocolate chips must be a passion of yours," he said.

Jenny slowly licked the side of her cone and watched his eyes darken. "Among other things."

He lazily appraised her, biting off a chunk of his ice cream, not content to eat it slowly and savor each taste. He'd made love the same way. But she hadn't minded. She'd wanted everything he could give her and more.

"You said something over dinner about going out of town?"

He nodded. "I'm flying to New York first thing in the morning. One of my LLCs is having problems with some deferred compensation issues."

Jenny straightened in her seat. Limited liability corporations? Compensation issues? Both had always been a special interest of hers. "What kind of problems?"

"It's rather complicated."

As if realizing what he'd said could easily be construed as condescending, Robert backpedaled. "I've found most women aren't interested in the boring specifics."

"Well," Jenny said, "I'm not most women. I'll let you know if you're boring me."

He stared at her for a long moment, then began to talk.

Jenny licked her cone and listened while he explained. Her brain shifted into high gear. Other than a newfound interest in sex, tax laws were her passion, and she didn't have to feign interest.

Every so often he'd pause and she'd ask a question. Without realizing quite how it had happened, Jenny had switched into accountant mode. She threw herself into the discussion of a topic that had been the main focus of her life for the past five years.

The streetlights outside came on and the after-movie crowd wandered in. But they didn't skip a beat. They just raised their voices to be heard over the crowd.

Robert, Jenny realized, had a magnificent

body *and* a fabulous mind. Here was the man she'd never expected to find, a man who turned her on physically and challenged her mentally. A man she could easily fall in love with . . .

Her breath caught at the realization, but she wasn't going to ruin the evening worrying about something that was not destined to be. She focused her attention back on the scintillating discussion.

Finally, after one of her questions—that actually ended up being more of an in-depth analysis of a tax loophole—he sat back and stared, as if seeing her for the first time.

"I can't believe you."

Jenny brushed a strand of hair back from her forehead and smiled.

"You're amazing." He leaned forward and took her hand in his. "Is there anything you're not good at?"

Keeping a man's interest.

The thought rose unbidden and Jenny shoved it aside. That kind of defeatism was in the past. Jasmine was too much a part of her now to give in to negative thinking.

Since they'd arrived at the ice cream store, Jenny had been more present than Jasmine, and Robert had seemed to like her.

So which one was she?

Jenny?

Jasmine?

Both?

Did it even matter? She'd had a wonderful evening, and if the look in his eyes was any indication, the best was yet to come.

Conversation during the drive back to the salon flowed easily. But Jenny couldn't have said what they discussed.

She was finding it difficult to concentrate. Part of that, she knew, was because of Robert's nearness. But mostly it was due to the mental volleying going on in her head. Would he or wouldn't he? Once they got to her car, was he going to ask her back to his place? Or would he play it safe and end the night with a kiss?

Jenny hoped he didn't decide to play it safe. He hadn't gotten where he was by sitting back. He was used to going after what he wanted. And right now she hoped he wanted her.

Her body still ached, stirred by the passion they'd shared in the storage room and the whipped cream discussion in the restaurant. Unfortunately it wasn't just about sex anymore.

She liked him. Really liked him.

He was fun and sexy and, best of all, she could talk to him about business without his eyes glazing over.

His depth of knowledge of accounting principles blew her away. She loved the fact that he had such diverse interests and . . . talents. It made him all the more intriguing. In fact, she had the feeling she'd barely scratched the surface when it came to Mr. Robert Marshall.

It was too early to know where their relationship was headed, but Jenny didn't want to blow it. So even though Jasmine told her to jump him, she resolved to play it cool.

"We're here." Jenny gazed at the dark salon and kept her face expressionless.

Robert pulled under one of the parking lot lights, turned off the ignition, and shifted in his seat to face her.

Tonight, in the diner, she'd seen a different side of Robert. And while she'd loved the fun, sexy side—what girl wouldn't—it was the man who'd talked about deferred compensation who'd captivated her.

The light cast mysterious shadows across his face, and she wished she knew him well enough to read the thoughts behind the enigmatic expression.

"Thanks for dinner." In the silence, her voice sounded husky and sensual.

"My pleasure," he said. "Next time I go there

I'm going to take your suggestion and check out the chocolate chip pancakes."

Okay, so he hadn't said anything about taking *her* there again, but at least he'd liked the place.

"Move closer." Robert patted the spot beside him.

With a delicious purr, Jenny obligingly slid across the seat, and he slipped an arm around her shoulder.

"Much better."

The combination of the scent of his cologne with the feel of his muscular body pressed against her threatened her resolve to let him take the lead.

She laid her head on his shoulder and fiddled with the buttons on his shirt. "What are your plans for the rest of the night?"

"My flight leaves early," Robert said. "I still have some reports to get together."

Somehow Jenny kept the smile on her face. She tilted her head. "How long will you be gone?"

"I could be back as early as Friday, but at this point it's hard to say." He brushed her hair with his lips and took her hand, twining his fingers through hers. "I'm going to miss you."

Though she found the sentiment touching,

Jenny forced a laugh. "Don't give me that. You're going to be so busy, you won't have time to think of me."

He chuckled. "You're probably right."

Her smile vanished. She tried to take back her hand, but Robert held tight. "I need to go."

"Not so fast." His thumb caressed the back of her hand. "Don't I get a good-night kiss?"

"Sure you have the *time*?" She tried her best, but the words came out with a sarcastic edge.

Appearing not to notice, he slid a hand up her arm, pulling her close. "Trust me. I make time for what's important."

Jenny opened her mouth to speak, but he slanted a gentle yet firm kiss across her mouth, and she forgot what she'd been about to say.

She drank him in, pulling him even closer, threading her fingers through his hair. Desire coursed through her veins, along with an overpowering emotion she couldn't begin to identify.

Robert changed the angle of the kiss, deepening it, shifting one hand to cup the back of her head, holding her still for the hot, sweet hunger of his mouth on hers. And, as his mouth devoured hers, she was consumed with want.

She wanted to feel the weight of his body against her. Wanted to taste the salty sweetness of his skin. Wanted to be back in that storage room . . .

"Robert," she moaned.

Slowly, almost reluctantly, he drew back from her, and her body clenched with hunger when his mouth left hers.

"Something wrong?" she asked, her voice husky.

"Not at all." Robert trailed a finger down her cheek. "What could be wrong? Great food. Great conversation. Fabulous kiss."

"I should be going." She paused and gave him a chance to protest. "Unless you want to . . ."

He captured her hand and brought it to his mouth. "I've got an early flight."

"I understand," Jenny said. But she didn't. After a fabulous appetizer in the storage room, he was turning down dessert? It didn't make sense. But then, Dodson passing her over for promotion didn't make any sense, either.

With that depressing thought in mind, Jenny opened the passenger side door and stepped out of the vehicle, still wondering where she'd gone wrong.

Ten

"What do you mean you didn't get naked?" Marcee's perfectly plucked brows pulled together. "That was the part of the story I was looking forward to hearing most."

Jenny took a sip of her bottled water and hoped Carlyle and Sons didn't bug their conference room. She and Marcee had been assigned to audit the books of the Naperville manufacturing firm, but so far they'd done more talking than anything else.

"So other than a little hot-and-heavy in the salon storeroom, what did you do all evening?" Marcee pushed back her chair and fixed her gaze on Jenny.

"We went to dinner, had some ice cream, and talked."

"About what?" The shock in her friend's voice

confirmed that "talking" had never been a major part of any of Marcee's dates.

Jenny, on the other hand, loved that one-on-one dialogue. She enjoyed finding out what made someone tick. Last night there had been no awkward silences, no lulls in the conversation, but for some reason Jenny was having trouble remembering what she and Robert had discussed. Except, of course, his business concerns.

Just remembering that discussion made her heart beat faster. "One of his LLCs was having problems with some deferred compensation issues. You know that's always been a special—"

"You talked accounting stuff?" Marcee groaned. "No wonder you two didn't do the deed. Nothing wilts a sail faster than tax laws."

"It was a very stimulating discussion." Jenny lifted her chin and dared Marcee to say different.

"For you, maybe," Marcy said with a wry smile. "But look at the facts. After that stimulating discussion he drove you right back to the salon and dropped you off."

"He had an early flight." Though her voice came out strong and confident, the longer Marcee talked, the more Jenny felt her newfound confidence ebb.

Up to now she'd felt good about the evening, happy they'd connected on more than just a physical level.

Not to say that she hadn't hoped he'd ask her back to his place for some . . . whipped cream. And, yes, when he hadn't, a tiny part of her *had* wondered if she'd been too much Jenny and not enough Jasmine.

Now she realized that it had been after the accounting discussion that he'd pulled back. Her heart grew heavy in her chest, and Jenny turned her attention to the laptop. The unexpected moisture in her eyes caused the row of numbers on the screen to run together and blur.

Damn men. Damn Marcee for reminding her what men wanted. Why couldn't great conversation be more important than—or at least *as* important as—great sex?

"I should have known that being myself last night would be the kiss of death," Jenny said with a sigh.

"That is so not true." Marcee's hand settled on Jenny's arm. "Any guy would be lucky to have you."

"Too bad they don't see it that way." Jenny blinked several times to clear her vision, then turned to face Marcee. "The only reason Robert was ever the slightest bit interested in me was because Jasmine is so fun and sexy."

"Don't sell yourself short," Marcee said. "Call it acting, call it getting in touch with your inner vixen, whatever. But it was still *you* in bed with him, not some nonexistent dead woman."

"Maybe." Jenny shifted her gaze back to the laptop and stared unseeingly at the screen. "I enjoyed the sex. More than I ever thought possible."

"And you shall enjoy it again," Marcee said.

"Not if he doesn't call."

"Give him time," Marcee said. "If that phone doesn't ring, you know his number."

"I couldn't do that," Jenny said.

"Why not?"

"Girls don't call boys." The words her mother had drilled into her since she'd been in middle school popped out of Jenny's mouth before she could stop them.

"Well, I hate to break it to you but we're not living under those poodle-skirts-and-sock-hop rules anymore," Marcee said with a laugh. "And you're a woman, not a girl. If you want to call him, call. If you want to have sex with him, have sex with him. There's only one thing you can't do."

Jenny lifted a brow.

"You can't fall in love with him." Marcee leaned forward, her green eyes dark and intense. "If you do, it's all downhill from there."

Robert double-checked that his travel alarm was set, slid beneath the soft hotel room sheets, and closed his eyes.

I wonder what she's doing now.

He groaned out loud. Since he'd left Chicago, thoughts of Jasmine had consumed most of his waking moments. Now it appeared she was creeping into the nighttime realm as well. He glanced at the clock.

Though it was after eleven Eastern time, it was still early enough in Chicago that she might be awake.

Was she lying in bed thinking of him? Goodness knows, even though it had been only a couple of days, he hadn't been able to get her off *his* mind.

When they'd concluded the business of deferred compensation today, he'd wanted to call and tell her that her instincts had been right on the money. But there had been no time. There'd been other issues to discuss, other meetings to attend, other business that took priority.

But there's nothing stopping me now.

Robert picked up the phone and punched

in the number he'd already memorized. He counted the rings. After five, disappointment sluiced through him, and his finger moved toward the disconnect key.

But at the last minute a sleepy voice said hello.

"Hey, it's Robert." He settled himself back against the pillows he'd propped up against the headboard. "How are you?"

"What time is it?"

"Ten-thirty, your time," he said. "I didn't realize you'd be in bed already. I can call back—"

"No," she said before he could hang up. "This is fine."

"You're sure?"

"Positive," she said. "Have you been having fun?"

Robert laughed. "We worked fourteen hours today. Started at seven. Had lunch and dinner brought in."

"You *are* such a wild man," she said in a low, throaty whisper.

"We got that deferred compensation issue resolved." Helen had been impressed by the depth of his understanding of the issue. And, thanks to Jasmine's astute comments he'd been able to toss out a few solutions to the problem. "Your suggestion about—"

"Stop," she ordered. "You didn't really call to talk business, did you?"

Robert paused. Actually, he *had* hoped to discuss some of the issues that had come up today and get her take on them. But he understood where she was coming from. It *was* late to get into such a heavy discussion.

"That's what I thought," she said with a breathless chuckle. "Let's talk about something important. Have you missed me?"

Robert smiled into the phone. She had no idea how much. "What do you think? I wish you were here with me right now."

"If I *were* there," she said with a light laugh, "you wouldn't be getting much work done."

"You don't think so?"

"Absolutely not," she said. "You'd be spending all your time in bed. I'd see to that."

His body stirred at the sudden vivid image of their naked limbs intertwined.

"It's a fantasy of mine," she whispered in a deep, seductive tone. "Going on vacation and never leaving the hotel room."

Arousal surged through Robert's bloodstream and arrowed straight to his groin. "Would you even bother getting dressed?"

"Maybe," she said. "Sometimes taking off the

clothes can be almost as much fun as what fol-
lows. Remember the night we met?"

"How could I forget?" He hadn't been able to
stop thinking about how she'd felt, how she'd
smelled, and most of all, how crazy she'd made
him feel.

"Do you remember what I was wearing?"

Robert leaned back against the pillow and
thought for a moment. "A tan skirt and a red
top."

He'd liked her in that outfit. And if he was
being honest, he'd liked her *out* of it even
more.

"I remember when you kissed me. I could
feel your hard cock pressed against my belly,"
she said in a sultry voice that sent heat coursing through his veins. "That's when I knew for
sure that you wanted me as much as I wanted
you."

His erection pulsed against the fly of his
boxers.

"You are a sexy, beautiful woman," he said,
his voice low and husky. "Of course I wanted
you. And when you started unbuttoning my
shirt—"

"One of us had to take the lead," she said in a
teasing tone.

Robert could see where this conversation was

headed and he realized suddenly it was exactly the direction he wanted to go.

"When your skirt fell to the floor," he said almost to himself, "I remember thinking that I'd never seen a more beautiful woman."

"Obviously you're a fan of Victoria's Secret lingerie," she said, her voice a sultry purr.

How she'd looked in that sexy red camisole and matching thong panties was permanently seared in his brain. Her breasts had been compressed and lifted until they threatened to spill from the red lace, while the smooth, firm skin of her derriere had been separated by a thin strip of the same lacy fabric. A groan rose in his throat. "It looked incredible on you."

"That surprises me," she said. "I seem to remember you couldn't wait to take them off."

"I wanted to do a lot more than that." Robert remembered how good it had felt when his body moved over hers, filling her, thrusting hard and deep as she arched beneath him.

"I'll let you in on a little secret." Her voice lowered. "I don't have them on now."

Heat flashed through Robert, making him ache with raw desire. He clutched the bedspread in his fists to keep himself grounded.

"I wish you'd been here to undress me. I like the feel of your hands on my body," she whispered. "Would you like to touch my breasts again?"

The blood in Robert's veins sizzled. The thought of touching that feminine flesh with his hands and tasting it with slow, leisurely licks of his tongue was almost more than he could bear. He shifted in the bed, which did nothing to ease his throbbing discomfort.

"Tell me what you'd do if you were here," she urged.

"I'd kiss you," he said.

"Is that all?" she asked in a sex-kittenish tone that both taunted and tantalized.

He'd planned on this being a quick call. Now he was determined to make it last as long as possible.

"I'd start out slowly. Like a fine wine, your lips are meant to be savored." Though Robert was sitting still, his heart began to race. He lowered his voice. "But there are other areas of your body just as sweet."

Jenny's heart started to gallop. She gulped. "Could you be more specific?"

"You have the most beautiful breasts," he said. "They fit perfectly in my hands . . . and in my mouth."

She cleared her throat. "I liked it when you sucked on my nipples."

The funny little noises she'd made had told him that much. "I liked it, too."

"And what you did with your fingers . . ."

A low, primitive growl rumbled up from his chest, and his fingers itched with the overwhelming desire to touch her again. To slide his palms up the insides of her slender thighs until his thumbs finally grazed the outer fold of her feminine flesh. He'd finesse her with sleek caresses before slipping one finger, then two, deep inside her. "You were so wet."

"I'm wet now," she said in a husky voice. "If I had on panties they'd be drenched."

Jenny didn't know what possessed her to be so bold, to say such a thing. Maybe it was because she was alone. Maybe it was the darkened room. Or maybe it was because it was the truth and she wanted some portion of their relationship based on honesty.

"I'm wet with the thought of having you deep inside me," she added. "I wish you were here so you could touch me and see for yourself."

Robert swallowed hard, which did nothing to calm the lust and need clamoring inside him. "I wish I were there, too. But that doesn't mean we can't have fun together."

"I don't understand."

"There's something incredibly exciting about a woman pleasuring herself," Robert murmured. "I want you to touch yourself."

"I—"

"Put your hands on your breasts," he ordered. "Roll the tips between your fingers."

Jenny hesitated, then succumbed to temptation. She tucked the phone under her ear, cupped her breasts in her palms, and grazed her fingers over the tips. She shivered as her nipples puckered and tingled.

"Talk to me," he said. "Tell me what you're feeling."

"I feel tingly," she said, her voice sounding oddly breathless. "And, well, tingly . . ."

She couldn't think of another word. Actually she was finding it difficult to think at all.

"Shut your eyes," Robert said. "Let your body tell you what to do next. Imagine that I'm there with you. That *I'm* touching you."

Closing her eyes, Jenny touched elsewhere, skimming her hands over intimate dips and hollows, all the while imagining it was Robert's hands caressing her. Her heart thumped hard in her chest as her body awakened. Her breathing quickened and her skin grew damp with every slick slide of her hands. A whimpering sound caught in her throat.

"Robert, please," she urged in a long, drawn-out moan.

The intimacy was amazing. His fingers tightened around the receiver and beads of sweat dotted his brow. For a moment it was almost as if he *was* there with her.

Inside her.

Easing his way deeper.

Groaning at the exquisite friction created.

Though intellectually Robert knew he was alone, he swore he could feel her inner muscles contracting around him. Just that quickly he found himself at the brink of climax.

But he denied himself, wanting her to find release first. Thankfully, she didn't make him wait long.

She gasped.

"Come for me," he murmured. "Come for me now."

"Yes . . . I'm coming . . . coming . . . oh, yes!"

Robert had always prided himself on his control, but hearing her announce her climax smashed his restraint. His own climax rose up and mingled with hers. His own moans joined hers.

Monsoonlike waves of pleasure rolled over Jenny. Her body trembled and her heart pounded in her ear.

After a moment, she collapsed back against the pillow, her heart rising and falling as if she'd just run a long race.

Dear God, had she really just had an orgasm over the phone?

If it hadn't just happened she'd never have believed it possible. When Robert had called, she'd instinctively sought to keep the conversation light so he'd want to see her again when he was back in town.

She'd never planned on having *phone sex*.

What had happened would make sense if she could say it had been Jasmine on the phone with Robert.

But that would be a lie.

It hadn't been Jasmine talking to Robert.

It hadn't been Jasmine having that fabulous orgasm.

It had been Jenny—all the way.

Eleven

Robert leaned back in his chair and took a sip from the mug of Black and Tan, ready for the evening to be over. It was almost midnight and the Irish pub in midtown Manhattan bustled with late-night diners and workers unwinding after a long week.

When Helen, the CFO of his New York operations, had suggested they grab a bite to eat after they'd completed the last of their business, he'd reluctantly agreed.

Robert had assumed Helen and Angie, her new administrative assistant, would be eager to get home after the meal and salvage what was left of the weekend. But after a leisurely dinner they'd stuck around and ordered drinks.

Angie especially seemed in no hurry. She finished off her second beer and signaled the waiter for another. She'd chattered nonstop over dinner while he and Helen had stifled yawns. But then Angie was only in her mid-twenties, so it was to be expected that she'd be ready to party when Saturday night rolled around.

If only she didn't feel the need to talk constantly. That's what he liked about Jasmine. She knew the value of silence. She—

"Robert?"

Robert looked up to find both women staring with an expectant air. While he'd been daydreaming about Jasmine, one of them had obviously asked a question. His money was on Angie. "Could you repeat that?"

"How early are you flying out?" Angie asked with an indulgent smile.

"Two o'clock." He'd deliberately scheduled an afternoon departure so he'd have time to finish up his business in the morning. But they'd tied up the last of the loose ends over dinner, leaving him free to take an earlier flight if he could catch one.

"Since you don't have to be up at the crack of dawn, how about the three of us check out a few clubs?" Though Angie extended the invitation to both of them, the young woman's gaze lingered on Robert. "After all, it *is* Saturday night and you know what they say about all work and no play . . ."

"Call me dull and boring." Helen pushed back her chair and stood, her hand covering another yawn. "All I want to do is get home, put up my feet, and read the paper."

Robert smiled understandingly and decided he must be getting older when Helen's scenario held more appeal than a night on the town. He pushed back his chair. "I'll get you a cab."

"A cab?" Helen laughed and motioned him down. "The subway stop is just around the corner."

There was something about the woman's independent stance and teasing smile that reminded Robert of Jasmine. An ache of longing filled him. God, he missed her.

While he'd done his share of dating and had even had a couple of long-term relationships, he'd never given any woman a second thought when he'd been out of town on business.

When those relationships had ended he'd thought it was because he'd been unable to devote the time to make them work. Now he realized he hadn't been *unable*, he'd been *unwilling*.

"Have a safe trip home." Helen grabbed her leather briefcase from the back of the chair.

"I appreciate the hours you put in the past few days." Robert included Angie in his gaze. "The hours you *both* put in."

Helen brushed a strand of silver hair back from her face. While her eyes were bright, lines of fatigue furrowed her brow.

"It was our pleasure," Helen said. "Just don't come back too soon. I need to rest up first."

Robert grinned.

Wiggling her fingers good-bye, Helen headed out the door, leaving Robert alone with Angie. Despite her invitation to go clubbing, he'd half expected, half hoped the young woman would leave, too.

But then, Angie seemed more determined than sensible. Taking another sip of his Black and Tan, Robert took a moment to study her.

He had to admit she was beautiful, in a wild gypsy sort of way. A cap of black tousled curls framed the oval perfection of her features. Her skin was smooth and a warm olive color.

She leaned forward, rested her elbows on the table and let her scooped neckline dip low. "Ready for some fun?"

Robert didn't know if she was coming on to him or simply being friendly. Playing it safe, he lifted a brow. "Fun?"

"Some drinking. Some dancing." She lifted her arms and jiggled in a manner he assumed was supposed to resemble a dance, staring at him through lowered lashes. "And after we're all partied out, I'll walk you back to your hotel. Maybe even tuck you in."

She giggled as if she'd said something uproariously funny and motioned the waiter for another beer.

Robert lifted the mug to his lips. She'd offered herself to him on a silver platter, and he needed to frame a polite, but firm, refusal.

It wasn't the first time an employee had hit on him. And it wouldn't be the last time he'd say no. When it came to business he had unshakable standards.

"We'll have a blast." Angie shifted from her chair to the one next to Robert, the one Helen had just vacated. Now that she was closer, Robert could see that Angie's eyes were glassy with an alcohol-induced glaze. She didn't even acknowledge the waiter who handed her another beer. "I guarantee it. The clubs here are fabulush."

"Another one for you, sir?" the waiter asked.

Robert shook his head.

"Onsh I finish this beer, we can go," she said.

Robert realized with a start that she'd taken his silence for assent.

"I appreciate the invitation," he said. "But the only place I'm interested in going is bed."

A flicker of surprise skittered across her face before her lips curved upward.

"I like a decisive man." She chugged the beer, pushed back her chair, and stood. "Your place or mine?"

Robert slowly rose to his feet. Good God, she really thought he intended to sleep with her. Even though he was her boss and at least ten years older.

"I have a girlfriend." The words flowed easily from his lips, which wasn't surprising considering he'd often used the excuse to get out of awkward situations. What was different was that this time they were true. Robert felt bound to Jasmine, in a way he couldn't begin to understand. And it felt good.

"So?" Angie lifted a shoulder in a slight shrug. "I have a boyfriend."

"You do?"

"Don't look so shocked." She trailed a finger up his arm. "Mike is deployed. He knows I don't do alone well. I'm sure it's the same for you. You're far from home. You get lonely. Your honey would understand."

Robert lowered his gaze and cast a glance at the hand resting on his coat sleeve. "She won't have to understand because nothing is going to happen."

He spoke slowly and deliberately so there would be no misunderstanding. Angie appeared to get the point. She removed her hand. "So is it no other women? Or just not me?"

"No other women," Robert said, his voice strong and steady. "The one I have does it all for me."

And what surprised him most of all was that the words weren't merely a last-ditch attempt to keep a predatory female at bay—he really meant them.

"You should have asked your new boyfriend to join us." Carol Carman passed the whipped potatoes to Jenny. "There's plenty of food."

Jenny stilled. "New boyfriend?"

"The one you went out with on Wednesday." Her mother stabbed at a green bean with her fork. "John and Jean Frank saw you at Nookies. They were going to say hello but they said you only had eyes for each other."

Jenny exhaled the breath she'd been holding, took a tablespoonful of potatoes, and passed the serving bowl to Annie.

"Why haven't you said anything about him?"
Because he's not my boyfriend, he's Jasmine's.

"He's just an acquaintance." Her voice came out casual and offhand just as she'd intended. Still, Jenny could feel her face warm.

"You really like this one, don't you?" Her mom's eyes sparkled and Annie looked up from the potatoes. "Bring him by. Your father and I would love to meet him."

Lloyd Carman kept his head down, appearing more interested in the food in front of him than in his older daughter's new boyfriend.

Jenny could only imagine Robert's face if she asked him to meet her parents.

After she explained that they didn't live in Phoenix.

And that her father wasn't French.

And that her name wasn't Jasmine.

"We've only seen each other a few times." Jenny shoved aside the guilt that niggled at her and kept her tone light. "I don't think we're at the meet-the-parents stage quite yet."

"That's smart." Her father looked up and nodded approvingly. "Too many girls try to rush a relationship."

"But you don't want to play too hard to get," her mother added, casting her husband a warning glance. "He'll think you're not interested."

Jenny took a bite of roast beef. She'd learned long ago that the best way to handle parental advice was to just nod agreeably.

"Is that all you're eating?" Concern edged her mother's voice.

Jenny glanced down at her plate. Next to the dab of potatoes was a small slice of roast beef and a pile of green beans.

"Are you on one of those new crazy diets?" A frown marred her mother's forehead. "I saw on the news last night that some of those can be dangerous."

"I'm *not* dieting," Jenny said.

"Jen's just being smart." Annie took a sip of milk. "She knows she'll never get a guy if she's old *and* fat."

Jenny paused for a moment, then burst into laughter. She might be the big 3–0, but lately she'd never felt younger.

"I've got a question for you."

Jenny looked up to find Annie staring. Her sister's innocent expression didn't fool Jenny. She'd seen that look in her sister's eyes before, and it always meant trouble.

"Is this new *acquaintance* of yours a good kisser? Does he give you tongue?"

Her mother's fork fell to the table with a clatter. "Anne Elizabeth."

Jenny couldn't say what got into her. Maybe she'd been hanging around Marcee a little too much. Perhaps she just wanted to put Annie on the hot seat for a change. Whatever the reason, Jenny leaned forward. She made her voice conspiratorially low, but loud enough for everyone at the table to hear.

"He's fabulous." Jenny purred the words and forced a dreamy expression. "And the things he can do with that tongue . . ."

Her sister choked on a green bean and Jenny stifled a smile.

"Jennifer. That is quite enough." Her father's eyes flashed blue fire, and the set of his lips told her if she'd been ten, she'd be on her way to her room without supper.

And she wouldn't be going alone.

Lloyd shifted his gaze to Annie. "Your sister has only been out with this man a couple of times. Why would you even ask something so ridiculous?"

Annie rolled her eyes, seeming not the least affected by her father's reproach. "Get real, Dad. This is the twenty-first century. These days girls do the deed on the first date."

Her mother's hand rose to her throat.

Her father's face turned even more red.

Annie giggled, apparently pleased with their reaction.

"I'm talking about decent, God-fearing people," her father sputtered. "Young women who would do such a thing outside of marriage, much less on a first date, don't fall into that category."

Jenny lowered her gaze to her plate and pushed the potatoes aside with her fork. Although her father's outlook was more old school than new age, for the most part Jenny shared his beliefs.

Regardless of how it might have appeared, when she'd gone to O'Malley's with Marcee she'd never planned to "get laid." She'd just wanted to flirt and have fun.

But from the moment she'd seen Robert across the crowded bar, she'd been a goner. Jenny had wanted him in a way she'd never wanted anyone before.

It hadn't taken a Phi Beta Kappa to know that a man as good-looking and successful as Robert would never be interested in a boring plain-Jane CPA. Lying about her identity had given her the confidence she needed to get to first base with him.

The trouble was, once she'd gotten there, first base hadn't been enough. She'd gone for the home run. And now she was in the mood to round the bases again.

Except what was she going to do about all these lies?

She shoved the worry aside.

"Mom, I'm going to head home after we clear the table," Jenny said. "I've got some stuff to do before tomorrow."

Annie perked up. "Would this *stuff* happen to include calling your new boyfriend?"

"He's not my boyfriend," Jenny told her sister honestly. "And I don't call him. He calls me."

"Good for you," her mother interjected. "Men don't respect women who chase them."

Jenny agreed wholeheartedly, but Jasmine met Annie's gaze and they exchanged a smile. Jasmine hadn't called Robert because he'd called her; not because "women don't call men."

On the other hand, he should be back now. Jenny wanted to give him a couple of days to rest up, but Jasmine was in the mood to seize the day . . . and hopefully the night, too.

That's why, as soon as Jenny got into her car, she took out her cell phone and dialed Robert's number.

Twelve

Robert dropped the suitcase on the living room floor and collapsed into the nearest chair. He'd snagged an earlier flight, only to have thunderstorms delay his departure. Then, when the plane had finally reached O'Hare, they'd circled for an hour, then spent another hour stuck on the tarmac. It had been after seven when the cab had deposited him in front of his condo.

Exhaustion seeped from every pore. The long hours he'd put in this past week had finally caught up with him. But he knew, even if he went to bed early, he wouldn't be able to sleep.

He was in acute Jasmine withdrawal and there was only one antidote.

Robert reached into his pocket and grabbed his phone. But before he had a chance to punch in a single number, it rang. Even though it was a private call, he had an idea who it was. Or, at least, who he hoped it was . . .

"Did you miss me?"

A flood of pleasure washed over him at the sound of her sultry voice.

"I did," he said. "In fact, I was just about to call you."

"Sure you were."

His lips lifted at the teasing tone. "I'll have you know, Miss Coret, that the minute I got home I pulled out my phone."

"Well, Mr. Marshall, I'll let you in on a little secret about those marvels of modern technology." Her voice lowered to a husky whisper. "Just holding them is not enough. Even the latest and greatest can't perform unless you push its buttons."

Robert laughed, even as his body stirred. He wondered if she'd intended the comment to have a sexual connotation or if it was merely his own need putting its spin on things. "Okay, point made. How about I hang up and give it a try?"

"How about *I* hang up and come over instead?"

"I'll be waiting," he said.

Only after the words left his lips did Robert realize how ungentlemanly they'd sounded.

"Actually, I can pick you up. Are you hungry? We could go—"

"I'll come there," she said. "The welcome home celebration I've planned doesn't work well with an audience."

Celebration.

Her voice had caressed the word, and he hoped her idea of a celebration was the same as what he was envisioning; long legs wrapped around his waist, bare skin heating bare skin . . .

He flipped the phone shut, and his anticipation grew with each passing minute. By the time the doorbell rang twenty minutes later, his body was on high alert.

She'd barely crossed the threshold when he reached for her. With a delighted squeal, she wrapped her arms around his neck and returned his kiss with reckless abandon.

"Wow," she said when they finally broke apart. "I'm happy to see you, too."

Robert's eyes drank in the creamy smoothness of her skin, the vivid blue of her eyes, and the golden halo of her hair. "You're every bit as beautiful as I remembered."

A flush of pleasure crossed her face. "You're looking pretty spiffy yourself."

"I missed you," he said, meaning every word.

"I haven't been able to stop thinking about our last evening together."

That time spent talking with her in the ice cream shop had been, for want of a better word, magical. He couldn't remember the last time he'd connected so completely with another person.

"It's been on my mind, too," she said softly. "I loved the appetizer in the storeroom, but I wish we'd been able to move on to the main course."

Robert looked at her slim fingers, her delicate nails. His gaze traveled up her arm, past the gentle curve of her shoulder to the hollow at the base of her neck.

An overwhelming desire to plant a kiss in that very spot pulled at him. But as much as he wanted to explore her sweet body again, Robert first wanted to make sure she understood that for him this was more than just sex.

"When I was in New York a really attractive woman hit on me," he said. "I wasn't even tempted. All I could think about was you."

"You are so sweet . . ."

He reached into his pocket. "I brought you something."

Her eyes widened. "A present?"

"You could call it that." Feeling more than a

little awkward, Robert stepped back. He slid a hand into his pocket, pulled out the package, and placed it in her hand.

For a long moment she stared at the small velvet box. Then, with trembling fingers, she lifted the lid. Her gaze lingered on the necklace nestled inside; a single stone, surrounded by filigreed silver, hung from a delicate chain.

"It's a necklace."

"A moonstone." He wished she'd say something more. While she hadn't taken her eyes off the necklace, he couldn't tell for sure if she liked it or not. It hadn't been expensive, but when he saw it, he'd immediately imagined her wearing it. "I saw it in a store window on my way to a meeting. It made me think of you."

She lifted her gaze to meet his, and the look in her eyes said it all.

He exhaled the breath he'd been holding and kissed her softly. "I'm happy you like it."

"Like it?" She gently caressed the smooth stone with the tip of her finger and shot him a brilliant smile. "I *love* it."

He took the box from her hands, feeling a flush of pleasure at her response. "Let's see how it looks on."

She stood very still while he fastened the

chain around her neck. Her skin was warm beneath his touch, and her closeness made it difficult for him to concentrate. It seemed to take forever, the tiny clasp awkward in his hands. Finally it cooperated.

She immediately moved to the large mirror in the entry and stared at her reflection.

"I think this is one of the nicest gifts anyone has ever given me," she said finally, her voice thick with emotion. "And I'm going to wear it," she added with surprising vehemence. "It's not going to sit in my drawer waiting for a special occasion."

Robert sensed the sentiment was somehow important—he just wasn't sure how.

"I hope you wear it often," he said. "And I hope when you do, that you think of me."

Their gazes locked, and for a moment time seemed suspended. Two bright spots of color dotted her cheeks. "I have a gift for you, too."

She fumbled with her bag, finally lifting out a can of Reddi-Wip. "I wanted to bring strawberries and champagne to go with the whipped cream, but I didn't have any on hand."

Though he'd been exhausted before she arrived, he suddenly felt like he'd just awakened after a long nap. "You know I've been up since five—"

"I understand." The light in her eyes dimmed. She lowered the can of whipped cream to her side. "It was just a crazy thought. Kind of perverted—"

Perverted? Robert pulled his brows together. What was she talking about?

She started to turn away but he grabbed her arm. "It's not a crazy thought. Or perverted. What I was trying to say is that I should be tired, but I'm not."

Some of the wariness left her eyes. But her smile remained tentative.

"In fact," he added. "The way I feel right now I could go all night."

He grabbed the phone from the side table and punched in a familiar number.

A puzzled look crossed her face. "Who are you calling?"

"Chez Gladines," Robert said. "For some strawberries and champagne to go with that whipped cream."

"I hate to be the bearer of bad news," she said. "Gladines doesn't deliver."

Robert merely smiled and hit send. Chez Gladines was an upscale French restaurant at the Pier. And while they usually didn't do takeout, he knew they'd make an exception for one of their principal investors.

"Philippe, Robert Marshall," he said. "I'm fine, thank you. The reason I'm calling is I need a large bowl of whipped cream, some strawberries, and a bottle of your finest champagne."

She moved to his side, her gaze fixed on his face.

"No, that's all. Can you have someone deliver them to my place right away? Great."

Robert hung up the phone, then called Harold and told him to send the deliveryman up as soon as he arrived. "All set. They should be here in a few minutes."

"I can understand the strawberries and champagne, but why the whipped cream?"

His gaze flicked over the small can. "I'm not sure that's going to be enough . . . for what I have in mind."

"Oh," was all she could choke out.

Heat pooled in Jenny's belly. Since the other night, she'd done nothing but imagine what she'd like to do the next time she and Robert were together. She should have known he'd have some plans of his own.

He slipped an arm around her shoulders as if holding her close was the most natural thing in the world. "I was thinking that while we're waiting we could do a few warm-up exercises."

For a second a vision of stretches and bends flashed before her. But the wicked smile on Robert's lips told her he had something far more fun in mind.

She kicked off her heels. "I'm ready."

His eyes seemed to glitter, looking more gray than blue.

Her heart picked up speed. She'd worried about this impromptu visit. Worried she might seem too forward. But the other night had whetted her appetite for more, and she couldn't wait a single second longer to be with him.

Now he was here, right in front of her, and she simply had to touch him. Emboldened by the longing welling up inside her, she stepped forward. "Tell me we're not just going to stand here all night and look at each other."

Robert chuckled and tugged her toward him. Stroking her cheek with his right hand, he pulled her chin up and covered her mouth with his own.

His lips moved lightly over hers, then trailed down the warm fragrance of her neck.

She shivered. Oh, how she'd missed him. Oh, how she'd missed *this*.

His hand moved slowly down her back, following the curve of her waist. With well-practiced ease, he maneuvered her zipper down.

The dress opened, and he slid it from her shoulders before moving to the clasp of her bra.

Three quick raps sounded on the door.

Robert swore under his breath.

She groaned, her breast straining against the lace, aching for his touch. "Tell them to go away."

Robert nipped her ear with his teeth and gave her a quick kiss. "I would, but I have definite plans for the whipped cream."

He was halfway across the room before Jenny realized that if she didn't move the deliveryman would get an eyeful. Holding her dress together, she scampered around the corner just as the door swung open.

She stayed in that position until the man from Chez Gladines was properly tipped and she heard the door click shut. Once she knew it was safe, Jenny stepped back into the room, holding her dress up with one hand.

A huge bowl of whipped cream sat on a silver tray surrounded by large, just ripened strawberries. A bottle of champagne sat in a bed of ice.

Jenny stared longingly at the mounds of luscious cream, telling herself she needed to be patient. But she couldn't resist the temptation. Leaning forward, she stuck her finger in one large peak and brought it to her lips. Her mouth closed around her finger, and she sucked the delicious sweetness.

A groan sounded behind her, and she turned to find Robert's gaze upon her.

"I don't know if I have the strength to play out your game," Robert said. "The mere thought of your body covered in whipped cream is about to do me in."

"My body?" She laughed. "You're the one who gets the whipped cream, not me."

"We'll see about that," Robert said with a devilish smile.

He captured her hand and she giggled, letting her dress fall to the floor.

His eyes darkened.

Keeping her gaze firmly fixed on him, Jenny reached for the clasp of her bra.

A knock sounded at the door.

Robert groaned.

"Maybe he decided the tip you gave him wasn't big enough," she teased.

Robert's gaze shifted from Jenny to the whipped cream and back. "Five seconds and he's gone."

Jenny barely had time to step out of her dress and slip back around the corner before Robert opened the door.

"Will." She could hear the surprise in Robert's voice. "What are you doing here?"

"We need to talk," Will said. "It's important."

"Is it Dad?" Robert asked immediately.

"No. It's—"

"Stacy? The baby?"

"It's not family," Will said. "Everyone is fine. This is about the . . . business."

"Oh," Robert said.

Trying to place the voice was driving Jenny crazy. It sounded so familiar. She'd definitely heard it before.

She eased to the edge of the doorway, close enough to hear both sides of the conversation without being seen.

"Can I come in?"

Jenny stole a quick glance around the corner. Dear God, he not only *sounded* familiar, he *looked* familiar.

William Marshall.

Robert's brother.

CEO of LDM.

Her knees turned to jelly and she leaned against the wall for support.

She'd done an audit on the furniture conglomerate when William had succeeded his father as CEO. Foolishly, she'd never made the connection . . .

"Now isn't good for me." Robert's voice was pleasant but firm, the same tone Jenny used with unwanted telemarketers.

Jenny couldn't resist. She peered around the corner and snuck another peek.

"It's Sunday night. For God's sake, what could be . . ." Will paused, and his gaze swept past the whipped cream, strawberries, and champagne before lingering on her shoes and dress.

"This is important, Robert." Will's voice hardened. "You know I wouldn't be here otherwise."

"Like I told you, I'm busy," Robert said.

"Send her home."

"No."

"No?" Will's voice rose. "I can't believe shooting your rocks off is more—"

"Not another word." Robert's voice held a deadly calm. "Remember she's the invited guest, not you."

Will's face reddened as if he'd been slapped, and Jenny almost felt sorry for him. She wasn't sure what he'd done to get on Robert's bad side, but she had the distinct impression there was no love lost between the two brothers.

"Sorry I bothered you." Will clipped the words, his face a stony mask.

"Will."

His brother paused, one hand on the doorknob.

"Call my secretary tomorrow," Robert said. "Tell her I said to fit you in."

Even from where she stood, Jenny could feel the tension. She held her breath, fully expecting Will to toss Robert's halfhearted offer back in his face.

It's what she'd have done. But Will just nodded, and a few seconds later Jenny heard the door close. She stuck her head around the corner.

Robert stood staring at the closed door.

"You can still catch him," Jenny said. "I'd understand."

"I want to be with you this evening," Robert said. "Not him."

"But he seemed upset."

Robert started to speak, then stopped and took a deep breath. "Let's not waste any more of this evening talking about my brother. Okay with you?"

It was a good thought, a noble ambition, but Will's appearance had already thrown a bucket of cold water on the evening. The fires of passion that had, only moments before, burned hot in Robert's eyes were now barely spitting embers.

Jenny understood. The heat in her veins had taken on a definite chill.

Robert knew Jasmine.

Will knew Jenny.

To paraphrase one of Gram's favorite clichés, the handwriting was on the wall.

If Jenny was smart she'd toss her cell phone in the river and never look back.

Because now it wasn't a question of *if* Robert would discover her real identity, but *when*.

Thirteen

Robert spent most of the next morning in meetings with his senior management team. He brought them up to speed on the New York trip and they shared what had gone on in his absence.

This was what he enjoyed most; the give-and-take of ideas, working as a team, but ultimately being the final decision maker.

During his years at LDM Robert had been increasingly frustrated over the fact that all major decisions related to the company had to go through his father for approval.

While Robert had respected his dad's authority, there were so many improvements that could have been made, so many opportunities that could have been seized, so many changes that would have solidified LDM's position as an industry leader, but Lawrence had refused to consider any of Robert's suggestions.

Even now many of those opportunities remained untapped. It surprised Robert. Will was a smart guy. Sure he'd had a lot to learn, but Robert had expected Will to make his mark on the company by now. To make *some* changes.

Robert frowned and shoved the thoughts aside. He had more important things to worry about than someone else's business.

Jasmine.

Last night had been less than satisfying, and he'd found himself thinking of her all morning. Will's unexpected appearance had put a damper on the evening. Jasmine had left less than an hour after Will, the strawberries and whipped cream untouched.

She'd said she had a headache, but he knew she'd left early because of him. He'd been distracted. Seeing Will, having him ask for help, had brought back old memories.

He didn't blame Jasmine. He'd have come up with a lame excuse and gone home, too. She deserved so much better than he'd given her last night.

Robert reached into his pocket, pulled out his cell phone, and checked his online calendar. The afternoon looked as horrendous as the morning. Still, if he skipped the conference call that began at noon, he should be able to squeeze in lunch.

"Mr. Marshall?"

Robert looked up to find his secretary, Margaret Reiker, standing in the doorway. Her ramrod-stiff stance and take-no-prisoners demeanor was testament to her twenty years in the Marines.

"Sir, your brother is on the phone. He insists on speaking with you."

Making sure Robert wasn't disturbed by unwanted calls or visitors was one of Margaret's main duties. She excelled at this task.

"He wants a meeting." Robert closed the cell phone and laid it on his desk. Though he'd told Will to call, Robert found himself irritated that his brother had once again intruded on his plans with Jasmine. If it wasn't for Will, he'd be on the phone with her right now smoothing things over. "Find a time to fit him in."

"That's a problem," Margaret said. "There is no time. You're booked until next Tuesday, and he refuses to wait that long."

Margaret's lips pursed together, and Robert could tell she didn't appreciate being challenged.

As tempted as he was to put him off, Robert knew that if he didn't deal with this now, his brother would keep calling.

Will had been that way even as a child. He might have been the worst player on the neighborhood baseball team but he'd made up in tenacity what he lacked in talent.

Robert glanced at the clock. Five minutes. That's all he'd give him. Not a second more. "Put him through."

A moment later, the phone on his desk buzzed. Robert picked up the receiver. "Robert Marshall."

"Rob." Even across the phone lines, Robert could hear the relief in his brother's voice. "I wasn't sure Brunhilde would let me talk to you. I called earlier and—"

"I don't have much time," Robert cut him off without apology. "I just got back from New York and I'm way behind. I'm sure you understand."

"Of course." Will's tone turned businesslike. "I'll keep this short and to the point. LDM is in trouble. Our cash flow's in the toilet. Unless something drastic changes in the next sixty days, we won't make payroll. I have a couple of ideas I want to run by you—"

"Will," Robert stopped his brother, seeing no need to waste any more time. "I'm not the one to talk to about this. I'm not involved. I haven't been for years."

"I realize that," Will said. "But you know the business better than anyone. With the exception of Dad and me, of course."

Dad and me.

Robert gritted his teeth. He'd wager even after two years away, he still knew more than the both of them put together.

"I'm sure the two of you can handle the situation." With great effort Robert managed to keep his tone civil.

"Robert. This is serious."

"That's why you're the CEO." Robert clicked on his e-mail account and let his gaze slide down the list. "It's your job to handle—"

"We may lose the company."

"What? How can that be?" Robert straightened in the chair, the e-mails forgotten. Once when he'd been a boy Robert had fallen from his bike and had the air knocked out of him. He'd always remembered that feeling. He felt that same way now. His fingers tightened around the receiver. "It was thriving two years ago. What the hell happened?"

"It's not the same market it was back then. Hell, it's not the same market it was last year." Will's tone held a mixture of defiance and weary resignation. "National Furniture is interested in buying. They're offering a decent price and we've had preliminary discussions."

Robert opened his mouth to tell Will he was crazy to even entertain an offer, that there were a hundred things he could do to turn the company around. But the old hurt at being passed over rose up and the words never made it past his lips. This crisis wasn't his concern.

"I don't know what you expect from me," he said finally.

"I thought maybe we could get together. I could bring all the financials. We could go through them—"

"I'm afraid there is no 'we' about this," Robert said. "This is your problem. You need to deal with it."

"But Robert—"

"Running LDM is *your* job, Will," Robert said, "not mine."

The silence on the other end of the line lasted so long, Robert began to wonder if his brother had hung up.

"So that's the way it is," Will said finally.

"That's the way it is." Robert wondered why he felt like such a jerk when all he was asking was that his brother earn his pay.

"Thanks for your time." Will's tone remained polite, but a distinct coolness permeated the words. "If we decide to go ahead with the sale, I'll give you a call. I wouldn't want you to read about it in the paper."

Robert hung up the phone. He'd been waiting for Will to screw up, knew it was merely a matter of time until he did. But he'd never wanted the family's ownership of the company compromised.

Surely Will wasn't serious about selling LDM. No, more than likely the few well-chosen words had been a ploy to get him to agree to help. Though Robert didn't doubt the firm had fallen on tough times, Will had taken responsibility for those difficulties when he'd accepted the CEO position.

While he wasn't proud of the emotion, in a perverse way, the thought of Will struggling gave Robert a sense of satisfaction.

When his father had turned the company over to Will, he'd told Robert he'd chosen the best man for the job.

Robert couldn't help but wonder if his dad still felt that way now.

"You want me to audit LDM?" Jenny did her best to keep the panic out of her voice. It had been one thing to audit LDM before she'd met Robert. But now that she knew the company was his family business, it was impossible. She couldn't go near the place.

Rich Dodson reclined back in his leather desk chair, his gray eyes cool and assessing. "Is there a problem?"

A hysterical laugh made it all the way to Jenny's throat before she swallowed it. Wrong? What could be wrong?

She was dead.

Do not pass Go.

Do not collect two hundred dollars.

Dead.

She cleared her throat and somehow managed to force an interested smile. "What's the reason for the audit?"

"The firm is on shaky ground." Rich tapped his pen against the desk in an irritating rat-a-tat rhythm that plucked at her already overwrought nerves.

Jenny gritted her teeth and waited for him to continue, resisting the urge to snatch the infernal Montblanc from his fingers.

"They don't want to sell," Rich said, "but they've had a viable offer and have decided to proceed with the preliminaries."

It made good business sense. A due diligence audit was considered standard procedure before a sale. And for anyone with enough assets to even consider buying the furniture giant, it would be a necessity.

Last night's unexpected visit came into focus. Had Will come by to tell Robert about the pending sale? Or to ask for help in saving the company?

But Will's reasons didn't concern her. She had her own problems.

LDM wanted her back.

Jenny's brows pulled together. That was the piece of the puzzle that didn't fit. "I always thought the buyer chose the accounting firm."

"They did," Rich said. "National Furniture hired us. I chose you to run front end on the audit for several reasons. Not the least of which is your familiarity with LDM."

"That audit was a couple of years ago," Jenny protested.

"When I spoke to Will Marshall, he mentioned you."

Most clients had trouble recalling her name the minute she walked out the door. But the way her luck was going, it only figured Robert's brother would remember her. And, unfortunately, she couldn't blame that fact on anyone but herself.

After she'd delivered her audit findings two years ago, the conversation had turned personal.

When Will had said something about being a former high school economics teacher, instead of keeping her mouth shut she'd mentioned that her father taught econ at Barrington High.

That had been the beginning of a quite pleasant, lengthy conversation. Who would have known it would turn out to be a problem now?

Jenny raised a shaky hand to her forehead. She didn't want to have anything to do with Will Marshall *or* his company. But if she told Dodson no, he wouldn't understand. He'd likely see it as insubordination and she'd be instantly out of a job.

What had Marcee said about good news? Jenny couldn't see how it could get any worse.

"I'll start prepping tomorrow." Feeling like a prisoner about to be executed, Jenny rose to her feet. "I have some paperwork to finish today."

"That'll be fine," Rich said in a dismissive tone, and Jenny headed for the door.

"Oh, one more thing."

Jenny turned, hoping against hope that Rich had experienced a sudden change of heart.

"I don't know if you're aware that Will's brother, Robert Marshall, is a very successful businessman in his own right. Seems like everything the guy touches turns to gold."

A sick feeling took up residence in the pit of

Jenny's stomach. She could tell where this was heading.

Shoot me now, Jenny thought. *Shoot me now and put me out of my misery.*

She nodded, not trusting herself to speak.

"I've tried numerous times to schedule a meeting with him, but I haven't been able to get past that Rottweiler secretary of his." Rich's lips pursed together and frustration blanketed his face. "I'm hoping you might have better luck."

"What do you expect me to do?" Jenny clasped her hands together to still their trembling.

"If you happen to see the brother around, introduce yourself, talk up the firm," Rich said, his gaze serious and intense. "I don't have to tell you, if we could land Robert Marshall as a client it would be a big coup. And there just might be a promotion in it for you."

Jenny stared at her computer monitor. She'd made such a mess of everything. What had she been thinking, telling all those lies? And the worst part was, she was beginning to feel that if she'd been honest from the beginning, Robert might have liked Jenny as much as he liked Jasmine.

Now she was going to audit his brother's company and all her lies were going to come crashing down around her. She needed to tell Robert the truth.

Maybe he would understand. After all, they were so good together. Even though she wanted to cling to that glimmer of hope, she wasn't going to kid herself. Once she told him, that would be it. Robert would be out of her life for good . . .

The musical ring of her cell phone pulled her from her reverie. She didn't need to look at the readout to know it was Robert.

The song continued to play, and Jenny flipped the phone open. "Hello."

"Miss me?" The deep voice sent a shiver up her spine.

"Who is this?" Jenny took a stab at humor, then ruined the effect with a slightly hysterical laugh. "Hello, Robert."

"You didn't answer my question."

Jenny paused. Instead of a flippant Jasmine response that was poised on the tip of her tongue, the words Jenny uttered came straight from her heart. "Yes," she said softly. "I have missed you."

"Good," he said. "I needed to hear that."

She caught the strain in his voice. "Bad day?"

"I've had better." He hesitated. "I know this is short notice, but I'd like to see you, and I wondered if you were free for lunch?"

For as long as Jenny could remember she'd worked through lunch.

Seize the day.

"I'd love to do lunch."

"Great," Robert said. "Say—"

"Yes?"

"I don't know what your schedule is like," Robert began, then stopped. "No. I'm sure it wouldn't work."

Jenny could have let the comment go, but she didn't. She was through regretting missed opportunities. "Why don't you tell me what you have in mind and I'll let you know if it'll work or not."

"Wouldn't it be fun to just chuck everything and spend the afternoon together at the Pier?" he said. "Of course I understand if you have appointments and can't take off."

Jenny found the uncertainty endearing. The knowledge that this would be their last time together made it impossible for her to say no. "Sounds like a good time."

"You'll do it?"

"Of course." Jenny smiled into the phone and took another sip of soda. "I'd do anything for you."

Fourteen

"You do not want to go on the Ferris wheel," Robert teased.

"I really do." Jasmine pulled a multicolored wad of cotton candy from the bag and held it up. "I'll give you a bite if you ride with me."

"I seem to recall that I was the one who bought that," he said with mock seriousness, enjoying the banter.

It had been years since he'd taken an afternoon off. His secretary had been furious and, knowing his tight schedule, Robert couldn't blame her. He still wasn't sure what possessed him to do it. But right now he couldn't imagine being anywhere else.

After a leisurely lunch at Chez Gladines, they'd wandered in and out of the shops at Navy Pier, holding hands and talking. He'd been surprised to find himself telling her all about his business and plans for the future.

Their time together had only confirmed what he'd already known; Jasmine was a great listener. Though he loved discussing his work, he hadn't wanted to monopolize the conversation. But each time he'd asked about her salon, she changed the subject. He finally quit trying. She was probably just experiencing a little guilt. He could understand. It hadn't been easy for him to play hooky, either. But it was turning out to be a perfect day.

When they'd come out of the last store, the sun was warm on their faces and Jasmine had proclaimed it a cotton candy day.

He'd willingly gone along with that request, but ride a Ferris wheel? He cast his gaze over the line filled with tourists and older women. Absolutely not.

"C'mon, Robert, be a sport." Jasmine trailed a finger up his arm, and he could feel his resolve weaken. "I've always wanted to kiss a boy at the top of a Ferris wheel." Her mouth turned downward in a tantalizing pout. "It never happened."

"Those boys were fools." Robert couldn't imagine any red-blooded male—no matter what his age—resisting her.

Just looking at her now made his heart beat faster. Her lips were glazed with the remnants of spun sugar, and he had the sudden impulse to find out how she tasted. The hell with waiting until they were a hundred and fifty feet in the air.

"You'll do it?" Her eyes lit up like a child who'd just been granted her fondest wish.

At that moment, Robert would have done anything she asked. "Of course I will."

He bought the tickets, and they moved to the end of the line snaking its way down the boardwalk. Robert took another wad of cotton candy from the bag. He looked up to find her staring, an indulgent smile lifting her lips.

"What?" He popped the sugary concoction into his mouth, savoring the appealing taste on his tongue.

"I'm beginning to think you like the stuff more than I do."

Robert started to deny it, then chuckled and raised his hands. "Guilty as charged."

"Wow," she said, widening her eyes in mock surprise. "The guy is not only sexy, but honest as well."

Robert hadn't been waiting for an opening, but since one had presented itself, he took a deep breath and plunged ahead, trying his best to keep his tone deliberately light. "How's this for honesty; do you know that I've never been the slightest bit tempted to take an afternoon off so I could be with a woman?"

A look of surprise crossed her face. "Really?"

Though he'd been enchanted by the intelligent conversation and her good looks, he hadn't planned to let things move beyond the jazz club. He didn't have time for a relationship. But every time he'd seen her, there had been that undeniable chemistry . . .

Every time he'd seen her, his feelings had deepened. And it was suddenly important that she know this wasn't some casual fling.

"What I'm trying to say is, I can't imagine my life without you in it."

"I thought you were too busy for a girlfriend." The strain around her eyes was at odds with her light tone.

"That was before you." Robert willed her to see by the look in his eyes that he'd never been more serious. "Before I realized what's really important."

"I realize what's important, too," she said, flashing him a bright smile. "That's why I'm riding the Ferris wheel."

Though he was a bit disappointed she didn't share her own feelings with him, Robert couldn't help but smile back. He'd never seen a woman so passionate about a carnival ride.

Especially a *Ferris wheel*.

It had been years since he'd ridden one. The last time was at the state fair in Springfield. He'd been starting middle school, and like most boys that age, he loved rides that were fast, scary, and high.

He'd hoped to go on many such rides that day. But by the time they'd made it to the midway, his father was in a hurry to get back to Chicago, and Robert was told he could pick only one ride. And he had to take his brother.

Robert had wanted to ride the roller coaster, but when he'd mentioned it to Will, fear had blanched his little brother's face. Robert knew if his father discovered Will was scared, they'd be riding the Scream Roller for sure. Lawrence Marshall had always been big on facing your weaknesses.

But Robert had not only been Will's big brother back then, he'd been his protector. So instead of holding his hands high in the air and screaming until he was hoarse, Robert had told Will he'd changed his mind, and they'd ridden the Ferris wheel instead.

He still remembered the look of gratitude in Will's eyes.

Will.

Damn. The conversation just before lunch still ate at him. While he'd been well within his rights to say what he did, he still felt guilty.

"Is something wrong?" Worry underscored Jasmine's words.

Robert shrugged aside thoughts of Will. He was not his brother's keeper. Will had taken the CEO job, and now he could damn well take the bad with the good.

"How could there be?" He slipped an arm around her shoulder. "I'm with you."

She tilted her head and looked up at him, batting her long, dark lashes. "Why, Mis-tuh Marshall, you say the sweetest things."

"They're all true." Without missing a beat, he slid his hand down, plucked a wad of cotton candy from the bag, and immediately popped it into his mouth.

"Hey," she protested, but the sparkle in her blue eyes told him she hadn't minded at all.

God, she was beautiful.

"You're all mine," he murmured. The thought made him smile. He pulled her tight, not able to put off kissing her a moment longer.

But just as his lips were lowering to hers, he felt a jab in his side.

"Do you two want to get on?" the older man working the ride barked. "Or are you going to stand there all day making goo-goo eyes at each other?"

Several teens behind them laughed.

Robert opened his mouth but shut it before speaking, knowing any unpleasantness would mar Jasmine's fantasy. Instead he shot the man a leveling look, letting him know he hadn't appreciated the comment.

Jasmine didn't seem to notice the man's curtness. Or, if she did, she wasn't bothered by it. Laughing, she grabbed his hand and slid inside the seat of the gondola car. He settled in next to her, placing one arm around her shoulder.

"When we get to the top," she said, lifting her hands as the bar clicked shut across their laps, "you have to kiss me."

He raised a brow. "Have to?"

"Have to," she repeated. She tried her best to look stern, but the twinkle in her eyes gave her away. "If you know what's good for you, that is."

His gaze took in her flushed cheeks, her windblown hair, and the sticky residue on her lips. An emotion he'd never felt before rose inside him.

"Don't worry." He gently brushed back a strand of hair from her face. "I definitely know what's good for me."

Jenny leaned back in the chair at the sidewalk café and pushed away the basket of tortilla chips.

After the Ferris wheel, they'd gone on the carousel, then stopped for drinks. She'd told Robert you couldn't have margaritas without chips. Now she wished she'd made an exception to that rule. "I'm not going to eat another bite."

"Hmm." Robert's expression remained serious but she caught the momentary twitch of his lips. "Correct me if I'm wrong but I think I've heard that before."

"Chez Gladines is known for their crème brûlée," Jenny protested. "And how can you *not* get ice cream and cotton candy when you're at Navy Pier? It'd be like going to a movie and not getting popcorn and a soda."

"You're right," he said. "Can't be done."

Until that dimple in his cheek flashed, she wasn't sure if he was teasing or not.

"It's a rule," Jenny retorted.

He just smiled, and she couldn't help but laugh.

Jenny grabbed a chip and took a sip of her margarita, feeling completely and utterly content. The sun shone high overhead and the sky was a brilliant, breathtaking blue.

By the looks of the crowded sidewalks surrounding the outdoor café, she and Robert weren't the only two who'd decided the Pier was the place to be on a beautiful May afternoon.

Reflecting back on all those years she'd kept her nose to the grindstone, Jenny had to wonder what she'd been thinking. A wave of regret washed over her. Why had she wasted so much precious time?

"Would you excuse me for a minute?" Robert pushed his chair back. "There's someone over there I know."

"Take your time." Jenny lifted her glass. "Margarita and I will sit here and enjoy the sun."

Robert rose and gave her shoulder a squeeze as he walked past. "I won't be long."

Taking another sip of her blended drink, Jenny watched him maneuver between the tables, and her heart fluttered. What was it about the man that made her feel like a schoolgirl in the throes of a rampant crush? Just looking at him did crazy things to her insides. And, try as she might, she couldn't take her eyes off him. From where she sat she could see she wasn't the only enamored woman. Every pair of female eyes followed him. Dressed casually in a pair of khakis and a cotton shirt, he couldn't have looked any better . . . unless he was naked, of course.

Jenny smiled and brought the glass to her lips. If she was a betting woman, she'd lay odds that she'd see him that way before the afternoon was over.

"Jen?" A shocked voice sounded off to her side. "What are you doing here?"

Jenny's heart plummeted and she almost dropped her drink. She plastered a smile on her lips and shifted in her seat to face her sister.

"I took the afternoon off." Thankfully her voice gave nothing away.

Over Annie's shoulder Jenny saw Robert talking intently to a man who looked to be in his early thirties. Perhaps an old college buddy? Or business associate? Whatever the situation, Jenny just prayed the two had a lot of catching up to do. "What about you? Shouldn't you be in school?"

Annie blushed, and her normally confident demeanor wavered for a split second. "Maddie and Fern and I cut out a little early. There's only a week left anyway."

For a second Jenny was tempted to launch into a lecture on self-discipline, to remind her sister that each day she wasn't in class was a day of learning lost. Instead she took another sip of her drink.

Lecturing Annie would take way too long and accomplish way too little. Besides, she needed to get her sister out of here before Robert got back.

"You couldn't have picked a nicer day." Jenny forced a smile. "You'd better go enjoy it."

Annie tilted her head and blinked in confusion. "Are you saying you're *not* going to tell Mom?"

"My lips are sealed." Jenny took a sip of her margarita and cast another glance in Robert's direction.

Drat. The two men were shaking hands. A clear sign the conversation was coming to an end.

"Look, Annie," Jenny spoke quickly, knowing there was no time to waste. "I need you to get lost. I'm here with a friend and I don't want to get into the whole meet-the-family kind of thing. You understand?"

Jenny's gaze moved to Robert and her heart gave a sickening lurch. He'd be at the table in a matter of seconds.

Annie turned around to look and her eyes widened. "Wow. Is that *him*? He's way cuter than any of the guys you've dated before."

"Leave." Jenny said the word between gritted teeth, keeping a smile on her face.

"Okay," Annie said. "But you have to promise to tell all later."

"I'm sorry that took so long. I—" Robert stopped as if realizing for the first time that Jenny wasn't alone. "Am I interrupting?"

"No, of course not." Jenny shot Annie a warning look. "She was just leaving."

Robert hesitated, and Jenny knew he was

expecting an introduction. When none came, he shifted his gaze to Annie and extended his hand. "I don't believe we've met. I'm Robert Marshall—"

"And I'm late," Annie said with a cheeky smile, totally ignoring Robert's outstretched hand. "Gotta go."

Robert dropped his hand to his side. He stared at the rapidly retreating figure for a moment before he sat down and returned his attention to Jenny. "I didn't mean to scare her off."

"I think she said she was meeting someone." Once Annie turned the corner and disappeared from sight, Jenny let out the breath she'd been holding.

"Who is she?" Robert asked.

Tell him. Tell him now.

But Jenny knew if she told him now, Jasmine would be gone forever.

"She's from my old neighborhood." Jenny gave a dismissive wave, surprised at how easily the lie slid from her tongue. "I'd have introduced you but I couldn't remember her name."

Robert accepted the explanation and took her hand. "Want to go back to my place and have some dessert?"

Even if someone paid her, Jenny didn't think

she could eat another bite. It wasn't just the food, either. Her many deceptions curled up like a lead weight in her stomach. She started to protest when she saw the gleam in Robert's eyes.

Her heart skipped a beat. "You're not talking about food, are you?"

His thumb gently massaged the palm of her hand. "What do you think?"

"I think I'm hungry, after all." She leaned forward and impulsively brushed a kiss across his lips. "Especially for what you're serving."

The rain beat a steady rhythm against Robert's bedroom windows. On the way back to his place from Navy Pier the sky had started to cloud up. By the time he'd pulled the Land Rover into the parking garage, it was pouring.

But once they were inside his apartment, the world ceased to exist. Nothing short of a hurricane would have garnered Jenny's attention.

All she cared about was *him*.

His touch.

His kisses.

His closeness.

"I suppose I should go home," Jenny said, but she made no move to get out of bed.

Outside the wind whistled and howled.

"And ruin a perfect afternoon?" Robert's

arm tightened around her. "Days like this are made for making love, for cuddling in bed listening to the sound of the rain, for laughing and talking about everything and nothing at all."

He brushed a lock of hair back from her face, his finger leaving a trail of heat in its wake. "What's the rush?"

The scent of his shampoo mixed with the clean smell of soap. An emotion she couldn't begin to identify rose up inside her. And, for a second, Jenny couldn't remember what *was* important enough to make her leave this man's arms.

Then reality came flooding back. Tomorrow morning she had to start preparing for the LDM audit.

With his brother.

"You don't want to drive home in the rain, do you?" he asked, his voice smooth as melted chocolate.

A whoosh of rain pelted against the window, and Jenny shivered.

Gathering up her courage, Jenny turned toward Robert. She couldn't put it off any longer. "I have—"

"No reason to leave." His breath was warm against her neck.

"You want me to spend the night?" She couldn't hide her surprise.

"I do," he said softly. "This has been a fabulous day and I'm not ready for it to end."

But it's going to end, Jenny thought, *whether we want it to or not.* Her heart twisted and tears filled her eyes. She turned her face into the pillow and determinedly blinked the moisture back.

"I'm not ready for it to end, either." And in that moment, Jenny knew that instead of dealing with the situation, she was going to ignore it. At least for a little while longer.

Jenny slid her hand through the mat of dark hair on his chest, caressing the sculpted muscles that tightened beneath her exploring fingers. "I didn't plan on staying over so I don't have a change of clothes."

"What you have on should work just fine."

"Right now I don't have anything on," she pointed out.

He lifted the sheet, and his gaze darkened. "You're right. You, my sweet, are nekkid as a jaybird."

Jenny rolled her eyes at the corny phrase. "What does that expression even mean?"

"Don't ask me." Robert chuckled. "All I know is that my dad loved to embarrass Will at family gatherings by telling everyone how, when Will was a toddler, he'd strip off all his clothes and run through the house at NAS-CAR speed, 'nekkid as a jaybird.' "

Jenny smiled, envisioning the warm family scene. Then she remembered that the little boy who used to run through the house "nekkid as a jaybird" was the man she'd be meeting with later this week.

Were he and his brother close? Did they spend much time together? "Speaking of Will, whatever happened with him? Did you two get a chance to talk?"

Robert's eyes grew shuttered. "He called this morning."

The closed look on his face and clenched jaw spoke volumes. Jenny didn't have to be psychic to know the conversation hadn't gone well. "Why do I have the feeling that you and your brother aren't the best of friends?"

Robert lay back on the pillow and stared up at the ceiling, resting one arm behind his head. "At one time we were," he said. "But that was long ago."

Let it go, Jasmine urged.

Jenny rolled to her side so she was facing him and propped herself up on one elbow. "What happened?"

Robert stared unblinkingly at the ceiling. A tiny muscle in his jaw jumped but he made no effort to answer.

Jenny laid her head on his chest and listened to his heartbeat. When the silence lengthened, she decided she should have heeded Jasmine's warning. But before she could backtrack, he started to speak.

"My family has been in the furniture business since the 1800s," he said. "The reins of power—so to speak—have traditionally been handed down from the father to the eldest son."

"And you're the oldest?"

Robert nodded. "Unlike a lot of my friends who felt pressured to go into the family business, I *wanted* to be a part of it. I loved the idea of continuing the tradition my great-grandfather had started; making fine furniture that would continue to bring people pleasure long after I was gone."

A faint smile touched Jenny's lips at the passion in his voice. Unfortunately, she knew that dream of his hadn't been fulfilled, and her heart had already started to ache for him. "Tell me more."

"I started working in one of our factories when I was in high school." His eyes took on a distant, faraway look. "In college I worked in the corporate offices, and after graduation I went full-time."

"What about your brother?" Jenny asked.

"Will never seemed interested," Robert said. "He helped out a couple of summers in college in the distribution center, but I don't think he liked it much."

Jenny thought about asking how Will had ended up as CEO, but she couldn't remember if Robert had told her that fact or if she just knew it because of the audit. She made an encouraging noise to let him know she was listening and let it go at that.

"My whole life had been geared around the assumption that when my father retired I would take over." His gaze remained on the ceiling, and it was almost as if he were talking to himself. "I never expected him to step down so soon or to turn the company over to Will."

"What happened?"

"My dad had some heart problems," Robert said. "Arrhythmias which are now well controlled with medication. The early retirement was a complete surprise to everyone."

"No, I mean, about Will. Why did your father choose him?"

"I don't know." Robert's voice was flat, unemotional. "One minute Will was teaching high school economics and the next he was running a multimillion-dollar company."

Jenny frowned. Robert was a hard worker. And from all accounts a great businessman. It didn't make sense that his father would deny him his birthright. There *had* to be more to the story.

"I'm surprised Will agreed to take the job." She followed his example and kept her tone even. "Especially since he knew it was supposed to be yours."

"I was stunned," Robert said. "I kept expecting someone to say it was all a big joke. But it wasn't. When I questioned my father, all he'd say was he'd picked the best man for the job."

"Ouch." Jenny winced. "That must have hurt."

Robert's lips twisted in a humorless smile.

Jenny's mind searched for something that would make this bizarre scenario make sense. "Had you and your dad fought? Were things tense between you before he retired?"

"We were always butting heads," Robert said. "He and I have very different management styles, and my threshold for risk is much higher than his. But the disagreements were never personal. And I respected the fact that as CEO, the final decisions were his to make."

Jenny raised a brow. Perhaps it was different with men. But with women, even if it wasn't personal to begin with, it usually ended up that way.

"At the time he retired I was trying to convince him to get into the Asian markets," Robert continued. "But he wanted to wait. As far as I know they're still waiting. It's got to be hurting their bottom line."

From the audits she'd done, Jenny had an idea what went into running a large, successful business, and she couldn't imagine a high school teacher stepping into a CEO's shoes successfully, not even one who'd taught econ.

"Have you talked to your brother about it?"

"It's his company now, not mine," Robert said. "My father made that very clear when he turned the company over to Will."

"He's never asked your opinion?"

"My dad was there to mentor him," Robert said. "Today was the first time—"

Robert clamped his mouth shut as if suddenly realizing he'd said too much.

"That's why he came over last night," Jenny said. "He wants your help."

And the fact that the company was considering selling told her Will not only *wanted* but desperately *needed* his brother's expertise.

Robert slid his hand through her hair and pulled her to him, scattering kisses down her neck. "I'm tired of talking about Will. There are so many better things we could be doing with our time . . ."

The feel of his lips against her skin sent delightful shivers of wanting coursing through her. And as his mouth moved lower, Jenny had to fight to keep her focus on the matter at hand.

"So are you going to do it?" she asked, her voice breathless. "Are you going to help him?"

Robert lifted his head and met her gaze. "Would you be disappointed in me if I said no?"

Jenny gasped as his finger slid up the inside of her thigh. "The only thing that would disappoint me is if you keep talking."

Fifteen

After finishing off a second glass of wine, Jenny leaned back in her favorite living room chair, feeling completely and utterly spent. The past twenty-four hours had been a roller coaster ride, and she had a lot to contemplate.

Yesterday she'd crossed another item off her list. She'd played hooky, leaving work in the middle of an audit to hang out with Robert. She'd never blown off her responsibilities like that before.

Still, the time at the Pier with Robert had been fantastic. And when they'd gone to his place . . . well, it had been another perfect evening.

That is, until Robert had asked if she'd be disappointed if he didn't help his brother. Jenny had known if Robert started seeing more of Will, her true identity would be revealed and her wild ride as Jasmine would be over. To her shame, she'd selfishly responded based on what was best for *her*, not him.

Jenny rotated the stem of the empty wineglass between her fingers and stared unseeing out the window. She didn't even know who she was anymore. Not only had she let this crazy deception go on for too long, now she was acting in ways that contradicted her own values.

As Robert's friend, she should have urged him to take that first step toward resolving his differences with his brother. Instead she'd kept the encouraging words to herself.

Still, a tiny part of her wondered if it wouldn't be a bit hypocritical to encourage Robert to reconcile with his brother when she hadn't done a single thing to ease the tension between her and Annie.

Shouldn't she have her own house in order before she started spouting advice and platitudes?

Jenny straightened in the chair, a curious energy filling her body.

Begin as you mean to go on.

Her grandmother had told her you could never go wrong doing the right thing.

It was time to put that belief into action.

"You're different lately." Annie shot her sister a sidelong glance.

For a Tuesday night the Woodfield Mall in Schaumberg was surprisingly crowded. Thankfully, they'd had no trouble finding clerks to wait on them, and both carried sacks filled with new purchases.

"Different?" Jenny cast a longing look at Ye Olde Chocolate Shoppe. "How so?"

"I don't know," Annie said. "More relaxed. Not so uptight."

The admiration in Annie's eyes and her approving smile took the sting from the words. Her sister's gaze lingered on Jenny's lime green shorts and tiny tee. "Your clothes are even better. You don't dress like Mom anymore."

"I'll take that as a compliment," Jenny drawled. "Although I'm not sure how Mom would feel about that comment."

"She's old," Annie said with her customary bluntness. "You're not."

Jenny's gaze returned to the chocolate shop. Annie was right. Jenny wasn't old. In fact, right now Jenny felt more like a kid than an adult. Impulsively she gripped Annie's arm, the bag of clothes in her hand flapping against her sister's side. "Remember the candy jar Mom used to have in the kitchen? The one we'd go through when she wasn't there?"

"I loved the chocolate-covered caramels." A smile of remembrance lifted Annie's lips. She sighed. "Those were the good old days."

For a second Jenny was tempted to remind Annie she was only seventeen. That, for her, the "good old days" were just a couple of years ago. But Jenny kept her mouth shut. On that topic, at least.

"Look to your left," Jenny said. "Can you guess what I'm thinking?"

Annie's gaze shifted from Jenny to the store, then back to her sister. "That it'll ruin our dinner if we get candy now?"

"No, silly." Jenny laughed. "I was thinking it'd be fun to go chocolate crazy. You know, throw caution and calories to the wind and get one of each kind."

It was another item on her list. Like kissing a boy at the top of a Ferris wheel. Her lips tingled as she remembered Robert's lips covering hers a hundred and fifty feet in the air. Though nothing could top that, Jenny knew the chocolates would be a solid second. "Can I count you in?"

"I wish you'd mentioned it sooner." Annie gazed longingly at the window filled with truffles. "I spent the last of my allowance on shoes."

Jenny waved a dismissive hand. "My treat."

"In that case"—Annie linked her arm through Jenny's—"let the feeding frenzy begin."

The shop had several small round tables, and Annie snagged the one closest to the door while Jenny ordered at the counter.

In a matter of minutes a large plate of assorted chocolates sat on the table between them.

Jenny popped a chocolate into her mouth and savored the rich flavor against her tongue. Though scrumptiously wonderful, it didn't come close to the taste of Robert's lips. "Mmmm. Sinfully good."

Annie bit into a cashew patty and sat back in her chair. A familiar gleam lit her eyes. "Speaking of things sinful, tell me about this new boyfriend of yours. I especially want to hear all about the sex."

Jenny nearly choked on an almond. Her sister was seventeen. A mere child. She shouldn't even be thinking about such things.

"Later." Jenny took a long sip of ice water.

"That's what you said earlier," Annie pointed out. "Three hours ago."

"There's not much to say." Jenny picked up a milk chocolate with a caramel center and handed it to Annie. "This is still your favorite, right?"

Annie didn't give the candy a second glance.

"Give me some credit. I'm not that easily put off."

Jenny studied her sister for a long moment, taking in the bulldog set of her jaw and her determined gaze. Clearly Annie wasn't going to give up until Jenny tossed her a bone. "Okay, but it's not that exciting."

Annie smiled. "I'll be the judge of that."

Jenny heaved a resigned sigh. "We met at O'Malley's, a bar in Lincoln Park. We've gone out a few times. He's nice but we won't be together much longer."

Annie bit into the caramel. "Why not?"

"Long story." Jenny picked up a chocolate-covered cherry and popped it into her mouth, wishing her sister would just let the subject drop.

"Take as much time as you need. There's no rush." Annie gestured to the plate. "It's going to take us a while to get through all of these."

The cherry turned bitter in Jenny's mouth. She had to force herself to swallow. Meanwhile Annie waited patiently for an explanation. "I may have lied to him about a couple of things."

"Ohmigod." Annie slapped a melodramatic hand to her mouth. "You're human after all."

"Very funny." Jenny shifted her gaze to the chocolates. "This is serious stuff, Annie. I really like him, but once he finds out, he's going to be so angry . . ."

Her heart clenched. Angry was an understatement. Once Robert found out, he'd be gone.

"I bet you're right about that," Annie said. "Most guys I know would be really pissed."

Jenny nodded and took another candy from the plate, not trusting herself to speak.

"Have you given any thought to taking the confession route?" Annie asked. "Throwing yourself on his mercy and all that good stuff?"

Jenny stared at her sister, amazed they were having this discussion. Amazed that rather than arguing or sniping at each other, they were talking. Like friends. Like sisters.

"You love him, huh?"

Jenny started to deny it, but realized she was tired of lying. To him. To Annie. To herself. "I do."

"More than you loved Michael?"

"I *thought* I was in love with Michael," Jenny said. At the time all her friends were either engaged or married. "Looking back I think I was more in love with the *idea* of being in love."

"I hear you clucking, Big Chicken," Annie said. "It's like last year when I thought I was in love with Tommy Andrews. Then I realized I just liked the idea of dating a quarterback."

It wasn't a perfect comparison but close enough for Jenny to know Annie understood. Jenny reached for another chocolate. "Michael and I were never right for each other. We were simply too different."

Annie raised a brow.

"He had very definite ideas about who he thought I should be. If I deviated from that image, I got shot down." Jenny looked at the coconut-topped chocolate in her hand and set it back down without taking a bite. Only lately had she begun to realize how much her former fiancé's censure had affected her self-confidence. "His comments really shook me up. I started to doubt myself."

"Maybe you were shaken because you didn't know who you were then," Annie said. "So you weren't sure if he was right or not."

Jenny pondered her sister's words. When Michael had called her perverted, a tiny part of her *had* wondered if he was right. Now, thanks to Robert's openness, she realized that what Michael had seen as perverted, other people saw as a normal part of expressing love. "I think you're right."

"You learned from your experience with Michael," Annie said in a surprisingly adult tone. "And you'll learn from this experience with—?"

"Robert," Jenny said.

"With hunky Robert," Annie said. "You're different because of knowing him. He'll be different because of knowing you."

"He won't be so trusting." The thought brought a deep sadness. When Jenny had approached Robert at O'Malley's, she'd never dreamed their interaction would go beyond the superficial, that the simple attraction would turn into so much more and she'd end up hurting him.

"That's why you might want to tell him the truth before he finds out," Annie said. "Even if he dumps you, at least he'll respect you for coming clean."

Her sister was right. Who knew such sage advice could come from a seventeen-year-old?

"How'd you get so smart?"

Annie flushed under the warmth of her sister's approval. "I listen to you and Mom. And Dr. Phil, of course." She lifted her chin. "I'm not the airhead you seem to think I am."

"No, you're not." Jenny met her sister's gaze, regretting how she'd treated Annie in the past. "You're one smart cookie."

Annie groaned.

"What?"

"You saw the Mrs. Fields cookie store on the next level, didn't you?"

Jenny smiled. There was something incredibly satisfying about being with someone who knew and accepted her as she was.

Especially when that someone shared her love of sweets.

Jenny glanced at the clock and leaned back in her chair. Though the tiny office she'd been given at the LDM corporate office was adequate, she was going stir-crazy.

The numbers on the computer screen had started to blur and her neck had a crick in it. Part of the problem was that she'd sat in the same chair since seven and it was now after twelve. She'd skipped her morning break, telling herself that the faster she completed the audit, the sooner she'd be out of danger.

But she couldn't sit another minute. Pushing back her chair, Jenny stood and stretched. This morning she'd spotted a coffee station down the hall. A donut and a cup of caffeine should get her through the afternoon.

She smoothed the wrinkles from the skirt of her navy blue suit. When she'd dressed this morning she'd deliberately gone for a blend-in look; serviceable shoes, navy suit, hair pulled back in a conservative chignon, understated makeup.

Jenny hoped if she kept her nose to the grindstone and didn't draw attention to herself, Will would forget she was there. Or at least not pay attention to her. When she'd looked in the mirror before she'd left home that morning, she'd smiled in satisfaction.

Completely forgettable.

The fact that this had been her normal look before Jasmine came on the scene was not lost on her. She smiled at the irony.

Grabbing her purse from the desk drawer, Jenny locked the computer screen and slipped out the door. At the moment the hall stood empty, and Jenny hoped it'd stay that way. At least until she got her snack and made it back to the safety of her hole-in-the-wall office.

She'd gone less than ten feet when someone grabbed her from behind. Jenny turned and stared into Robert's blue eyes. Her world spun like an out-of-control Tilt-A-Whirl.

She turned hot.

She turned cold.

She opened her mouth to speak but no words came out.

Was this a low-blood-sugar hallucination, or had her worst fear come to pass?

"What are you doing here?" Robert's brows pulled together in a puzzled frown. His gaze dropped to her toes, then traveled the length of her body. "And why are you dressed like that?"

Jenny blinked.

He didn't disappear.

She blinked again.

Still there.

And unfortunately still waiting for an answer.

"I was looking for you," she said finally, forcing a bright smile.

Surprise skittered across his face. "How'd you know I was here?"

Good question. Now if she only had an equally good response. If only she'd had her coffee and donut *before* he'd seen her . . .

"My secretary was the only one who knew I was coming here today."

Thank you, God.

"Actually your secretary was the one who told me." Jenny nodded her head for extra emphasis. "Of course, I didn't know where exactly you'd be, so I've been wandering the halls—"

"Margaret told you where I was?"

Something about the way he said the words told Jenny that Margaret wasn't a chatty person. Definitely not the kind of secretary to spill secrets.

"She didn't want to," Jenny said. "I wormed it out of her."

The ease with which the lie slid from her tongue took her by surprise. And it sounded surprisingly sincere. If she didn't know better, she'd be tempted to believe the story herself. Robert, however, didn't seem quite so gullible.

His frown deepened, and a sense of unease crept up her spine. But she'd dug herself in so deep, she saw no alternative but to go deeper.

"That secretary of yours is one scary woman." Jenny pretended to shiver. "Anyone ever tell you that?"

It was a calculated risk. For all she knew the woman could be a tight-lipped sixty-year-old grandmother who sewed teddy bears and visited the sick in her spare time. But his few pointed remarks had led her to think otherwise.

His grin told her that she'd hit the mark. "More than once."

The tightness gripping Jenny's shoulders eased. So far, so good. "Why are you here anyway?"

Her father had always said the best defense was a good offense. While he'd been talking about football when he'd said it, she decided to take the advice and run with it.

"Did you decide to help your brother after all?" she asked, unable to stop the hope that welled up inside her from spilling over into her words.

Robert shook his head. "I was on my way home when my father called and asked me to drop off some old papers I had. How about you?"

Voices echoed from the far end of the hall, and Jenny realized the people—whoever they were—would soon be rounding the corner.

She grabbed Robert's hand and pulled him into the office she'd just left, letting the door fall shut behind them.

"Jasmine." He pulled his hand from hers and took a step back. "What the hell is going on here?"

Her mind raced, considering and discarding various explanations with rapid-fire precision before settling on one.

Jenny took a deep breath, unbuttoned the jacket of her suit coat, and took a step toward him. "Remember my Ferris wheel fantasy?"

Desire warred with suspicion in his eyes. His gaze lowered to her lips. "I remember."

"Well, I have another fantasy. I call this one the CEO and the secretary."

Robert raised a puzzled brow.

"Desktop sex," Jenny blurted out. "Have you ever thought about it?"

His eyes widened for a split second before he shook his head. She didn't need 20/20 vision to see resistance in the set of his jaw. But to make the offer believable, she couldn't give up. Not yet, anyway.

Jenny moved closer and lowered her voice to a sultry purr. "Be a sport. Don't say no without at least considering it."

"Jas—"

"Picture it." In her mind the scenario suddenly came alive. "I'm a shy working girl needing to be coaxed out of a boring, humdrum lifestyle. You're the handsome young executive who'll bring me out of my shell."

She wrapped her arms around him, sliding her hands across his back, feeling the muscles tighten beneath her exploring fingers.

"We wouldn't have to undress completely," she whispered in his ear, getting swept up in her own fantasy. "You could leave on your tie."

He groaned, and she could feel a stir against her belly. His breath quickened. His eyes darkened. For a moment she was convinced he was going to sweep the papers off the desktop and make mad, passionate love to her.

Her body quivered in anticipation, her chest rising and falling.

But he pulled away and raked a hand through

his hair. "I can't," he said, his voice tight with strain. "Not that I don't want to . . . I just can't."

The smart thing would be to take the out he was offering, but the fantasy she'd woven had stirred her senses, and desire made her reckless.

"C'mon, Robert." Her fingers moved to the buttons on her blouse. "Just a quickie."

Determination warred with desire, and for a split second she thought he'd changed his mind. Then he shook his head.

"I've never mixed business with pleasure." His words were firm, his expression resolute. "I won't start now. Especially not in my father's office building."

A month ago she'd never have considered what she was proposing. Now her body ached with disappointment, and she was sure her frustration showed on her face.

"Give me your address," he urged. "I'll come over tonight and make it up to you. I promise."

Jenny shook her head. "It'll be easier if I come to your place."

His gaze remained focused on her lips. "Eight o'clock?"

"Works for me," she said.

"I'd better go." But even after the words left his mouth, Robert made no move to leave.

Her heart beat an unsteady rhythm in her

chest. A languid warmth filled her limbs at the look in his eyes.

"Can I at least get a good-bye kiss?" Jenny caressed her lips with the tip of her tongue. "After all, I did come all the way over here for nothing."

Robert started to shake his head, then stopped. "Oh, what the hell."

He hadn't planned on kissing her. If he'd thought about it, he would have talked himself out of it, would have reminded himself of all the good, solid reasons he shouldn't kiss her in his father's building, but there she was, her mouth all soft and warm and inviting.

His tongue teased the fullness of her lower lip, coaxing her to open to him, sweeping inside when she did.

Her hands came up and her fingers curled around the lapels of his suit coat as she leaned into the kiss, her tongue fencing with his, a slow, delicious thrust and slide that soon had his pulse hammering in his veins.

Ignoring the muffled voice inside his head that suggested this might not be a good idea, Robert angled his head to deepen the kiss. Other than his mouth on hers, he didn't touch her. Some remnant of reason told him that if he put his hands on her, he wasn't going to be able to resist the urge to find out just what she was—

or wasn't—wearing under that business suit.

It was the very strength of his desire to do just that, to open her jacket and slide his hand up under that blouse, to curve his fingers around the sweet weight of her breast, that made Robert draw back. "I should be going."

She raised a finger to her lips, looking slightly dazed . . . and incredibly appealing. "I suppose you're right."

He started toward the door, then turned back. "Tonight at eight."

She smiled but made no attempt to follow him out.

His gaze swept the small office, taking in the laptop on power save, the desk littered with papers. They'd been lucky. The employee must be at lunch. But enough time had elapsed that he or she should be returning any minute.

"You might not want to linger." Robert gestured toward the briefcase on the floor. "Whoever has this office probably wouldn't approve of us being in here. And I wouldn't want you to get in any trouble."

"Me, either," she said. "The last thing I need is more trouble."

Trouble, Jenny decided, should be her middle name.

She left the office right after Robert, but when she turned in the opposite direction she found herself face to face with Rich Dodson.

From the frying pan into the fire.

"Wasn't that Robert Marshall?" Rich craned his neck to see over her shoulder. His eyes gleamed with barely contained excitement.

Jenny thought about denying it. After all, what was one more lie? But it would be pointless. Rich obviously knew what Robert looked like, and the odds that he'd believe she'd been in the LDM corporate offices talking to a Robert Marshall look-a-like would be miniscule.

"You asked me to talk to him," Jenny said.

"Did he seem receptive?" Rich was practically salivating.

Jenny's lips tingled and her body ached with need. The heat of Robert's barely restrained passion had told her if they'd been at his place, they'd be in bed right now. She nodded. "I'd say he was receptive."

"Fabulous," Rich said. "I'll call him on my way back to the office. After all, I'm sure he has specific questions that you couldn't answer—"

"I'd hold off a few days," Jenny said. "He just got back from New York and I know he's swamped. Give him a week or so. I've planted the seed. Let it germinate."

She held her breath as Rich considered her suggestion.

"You're right," he said finally. "I don't want to undo the good you've done."

Jenny nodded and realized the ticking clock had gone silent. Time had run out. She had no choice. She had to tell Robert the truth before Rich or Margaret got to him.

Tonight, she thought. *It has to be tonight.*

Pain gripped her heart in a stranglehold, but she forced herself to breathe. Forced her eyes to remain dry. Forced herself to stay strong. She couldn't fall apart now. Not with Rich's eagle eyes on her.

"Did you come to see how I was doing?" Jenny asked when the silence lengthened.

"I was in the building and thought I'd say hello to Will," Rich said. "But apparently he's out of town and not due back until tomorrow."

Jenny breathed a sigh of relief, thankful at least one thing was going her way. "That's too bad."

"I was hoping we could all go to lunch," Rich said. "I knew it was a long shot but I thought it was worth a try."

"Lunch?" Jenny could barely get the word past the lump in her throat.

"Don't worry. There will be other opportunities. I'll make sure of it," Rich said. "Heck, maybe we'll even get the brother to come along."

Sixteen

Jenny pulled into the parking garage of Robert's condominium at ten after eight. She'd thought about not coming at all. But Jenny Carman wasn't a coward.

A liar, yes.

A coward, no.

The doors to the lobby opened, and the first thing she saw was Robert. Their eyes met, and her heart skipped a beat.

It somehow seemed fitting that he should be wearing the same blue button-up shirt he'd worn on their first "date." After all, tonight they would come full circle; the beginning to the end. She took a deep, steadying breath and resisted the sudden urge to throw herself into his arms and cling to him.

"You didn't have to wait down here for me,"

Jenny said. Thankfully, her voice came out strong and steady.

"I worried you weren't coming," he said, his expression unusually serious. "I hope you understand about today. It wasn't that I didn't appreciate the gesture. It's that—"

"Shhh—" Jenny placed her fingers against his lips. "I understood. And I'm sorry I'm late. Traffic was especially bad this evening."

Robert searched her eyes, and whatever he saw there seemed to allay his fears.

The elevator door opened and he followed her inside. He didn't even wait for the door to completely shut before he slipped his arm around her shoulders.

"This is much better. You. Me. Safe terrain." Robert heaved a satisfied sigh. "Have I told you yet how wonderful you smell?"

"It's a new scent." Jenny tilted her head back, but instead of inhaling the fragrance, he nuzzled her neck.

He didn't stop there. Scattering kisses down her throat, he pulled her closer still. Though she wanted nothing more than to give in to the desire mounting inside her, tonight they had to talk. "Robert, stop. I have something to tell you."

She tried to twist away but he held her

securely. His torso was as hard as iron, and she could feel his muscles beneath the fabric of his shirt. And low against her abdomen and belly, the hot, leaping pressure of masculine flesh.

The elevator dinged.

"Robert, let go." Jenny pushed against his chest. "The door is going to open any minute."

He grinned and tightened his embrace. "Kiss me first."

"Let me go," she repeated. But even to her own ears the words held little conviction.

"Now is that any way to act after your performance this morning?" His smile was so boyish and mischievous, she had to laugh. And even as she laughed, her body responded to his closeness.

What would be so wrong with one kiss?

Ignoring the warning in her head, Jenny slid her fingers around the back of his neck and pulled his head down, her lips softening with anticipation—

The elevator dinged again and slowed to a stop. Jenny jerked back, and this time Robert let her go. She barely had time to smooth her disheveled hair and move to the opposite side of the elevator when the door slid open.

The marbled hall was empty and silent as a tomb.

"I told you there was nothing to worry about," Robert said, the dimple in his left cheek flashing.

If only that were true . . .

He opened the door to his place and motioned her inside. "I still can't believe I ran into you at LDM. I was going to call and tell Margaret that you found me but she's gone until Friday."

This was it. An opening. A chance to come clean. To explain that she'd never even met his secretary. That the convoluted story was just another one of her many lies.

"Robert," she said. "I really need to talk to you about something—"

"Sweetheart, forgive me, but I don't want to talk tonight." His breath was warm as he spoke softly into her ear. "Not about work. Not about Will. Not about anything serious."

"But—"

This time it was *his* fingers that pressed *her* lips closed. "Indulge me."

If only she *could* indulge him, give in to the desire heating her veins. Pretend it was only she and he and nothing else mattered, nothing else existed. But it was that attitude that had gotten her into her current predicament.

No, regardless of how nicely he asked, she

couldn't go along with his request. "There's so much I have to say—"

"Not now." Fatigue edged his brow, and his words held a heart-tugging desperation. "I need you in my arms."

She could feel her resolve waver.

"One more kiss." Robert pushed her hair gently back from her face and brushed her lips with his. "Or maybe two."

"Okay. One—"

Robert didn't even wait for the words to leave her lips. He kissed her again, longer this time, letting his mouth linger. It was still as sweet, still as gentle.

You have to let him know. Now.

Jenny opened her mouth to confess but when his hands covered her breasts, the words died on her lips. And when he opened her shirt and his mouth replaced his hands, she couldn't even remember what she'd been about to say. When she finally came up for air, several hours had passed and she was naked.

"Robert," she said, once again gathering her courage. "Remember when I said I had something to tell you?"

His hand slid beneath the sheet and cupped her breast in one hand, his thumbnail scraping the hard tip. "Remember when I said I can never get enough of you?"

She shuddered at the huskiness in his voice, the warmth of his breath on her cool skin, the touch of his hand.

Had anything ever felt quite so good? Or so right?

Back and forth his thumbnail went, sending spirals of heat coursing through her blood until she couldn't stand it any longer. Jenny wanted him to burn with the same fire that consumed her. She reached for him, stroking him gently at first, then more aggressively.

He moaned, and she substituted her mouth for her hand. His breathing grew harsh.

Though they'd made love several times already, she wanted him inside her again. Impatiently, Jenny cast the sheet aside and moved over him. Wet with desire, she writhed against him until she found just the right position. In a single downward movement, she impaled herself.

"Yes," he gasped.

She moved rhythmically, slowly at first, then faster. His hands reached up and closed over her breasts, rolling the taut nipples between his fingers until she found herself begging for his mouth.

It took only one touch of his lips. He'd barely

started to suckle when she exploded into a million pieces. But she didn't stop. She continued to move against him until he lost himself inside her.

Now completely spent, Jenny remained sprawled across his body. She pressed her mouth against his neck and let her lids drift shut . . .

When she opened her eyes the room was bathed in moonlight. With great care she rolled off him onto the soft mattress. He didn't even stir.

It was late. But Jenny was in no hurry to leave. Instead of searching for her clothes, Jenny propped herself up on her elbow and studied Robert's sleeping face. At thirty-four, he was the most handsome man she'd ever known. With legs that were long and powerful, lean hips, and muscular shoulders, he looked more like an athlete than a successful businessman. Or maybe, she thought as she brushed a lock of dark hair gently from his forehead, a *GQ* model.

Though it might have been this package that initially caught her eye, from the beginning there had been something else; an intense awareness of him as a man, yes, but some indefinable something that drew her to him. Marcee thought it was lust, pure and simple, built up from years of doing without. But Jenny certainly hadn't been doing without since they'd met, and the attraction between them was still as strong as it had been that first night.

"How can I tell you good-bye?" she whispered, knowing full well there was no good answer to the question that haunted her thoughts.

Tomorrow. She'd tell him tomorrow.

Robert stirred and opened his eyes.

She forced a tremulous smile.

"You look awfully serious." Robert's voice might have been husky with sleep but his blue eyes were as clear as if he'd slept ten hours instead of ten minutes.

"I was thinking about the drive home." It wasn't really a lie. She dreaded the long trek to the suburbs, especially in the middle of the night.

"Then stay"—Robert's head lowered to her breast and his tongue traced a tantalizing path around her nipple—"and we can have some more fun."

His lips closed and gently sucked while his hand moved between her legs. The desire that she'd thought had been already sated for the night surged again stronger than ever.

"Oh, Rob." Jenny arched back, his touch

sending arrows of fire shooting through her body, through her blood, to land molten and burning deep inside her. "You're not playing fair."

A wicked laugh was his only response.

Robert stretched out in bed, his fingers locked behind his head. Jasmine had barely left, and he already missed her.

It wasn't just the feel of her body cuddled against him that he missed, it was *she*. He liked laughing with her, talking with her, simply being with her.

"I'm in love with her."

The words sounded strange when he said them aloud. Strange, but incredibly right. They'd come to his lips more than once during the course of the evening, but the time hadn't seemed right for such a declaration.

Over the years, Robert had watched his friends, even his little brother, fall in love, and wondered if it would ever be his turn. Now, incredibly, it had happened to him and he was going to seize the moment.

She said she wanted to talk. Well, he had a lot to say, too. This weekend he'd take her somewhere romantic. He'd make sure the restaurant had all her favorite foods. Then, over a glass of the finest wine, he'd declare his love and ask her to marry him.

He hoped she wouldn't think he was moving too fast. After all, time-wise, their relationship was still fairly new. But while he might have dated other women longer, he'd never gotten to know them the way he knew Jasmine. She was an open book, and what he felt for her was real and true.

The only question was, did she feel the same? The look in her eyes and the way she responded to his touch seemed to say she did.

Robert grinned. He was one lucky guy.

He glanced at the clock. Now, if she would only call and tell him she'd made it home safely, everything would be perfect.

Jenny pulled onto the freeway and headed for the northern suburbs.

How could she have left his condo without telling him the truth? She'd promised herself tonight would be the night the lies would end.

Still, it wasn't entirely her fault. He'd seemed as desperate as she to wring every last ounce of pleasure from the evening. Every time she'd opened her mouth to confess, he'd stopped her words with a kiss.

There had been heat. And tenderness. And

something that felt suspiciously like—dare she say?—love.

Jenny swallowed the sob that welled in her throat. It wasn't fair. He was the man of her dreams, and now, just because of a few lies, those dreams would be snatched away.

Okay, so maybe it was more than a *few* lies. But regardless of what she called herself or did for a living, she was still the person Robert had come to know and . . . love. Jasmine was a part of her, not a separate entity.

Maybe if she explained that to Robert, he'd understand. It'd be asking a lot, she knew, but if he loved her even half as much as she loved him, surely he could find it in his heart to forgive and forget?

Her fingers tightened around the steering wheel. Tomorrow. Even if he wasn't in the mood to talk. Even if he tried to distract her. Even if—

The car jerked to the right with sudden force. Jenny gasped and tightened her hold on the steering wheel.

Bump . . . bump . . . bump.

A sick feeling filled Jenny's stomach. She eased her foot off the accelerator and steered the car to the side of the road.

Though the freeway was lit, this stretch of

pavement was unusually dark. Casting a quick glance around, Jenny unlocked her door and stepped out of the car.

Her heart sank at the sight of what was left of her rear tire. Mere strips of rubber surrounded the rim. Thankfully she had a spare in the trunk.

Her father had taught both her and Annie how to change a flat, but Jenny had never put the skill to use. The one time she'd tried, she hadn't been able to get the lug nuts loosened and the old tire off.

She had no reason to think tonight would be any different.

Thank heaven for cell phones.

Jenny slid back behind the wheel, and after making sure her windows were up and the doors locked, she pulled out her cell phone and her insurance card. Good thing she'd spent the extra money for roadside assistance.

Fifteen minutes later she bit back an expletive. It only figured that the one time she needed help, there'd be a multicar accident in the vicinity.

She put her name on a wait-list for a tow truck and called her parents. Her heart dropped when the call went directly to voice mail.

Jenny left a detailed message but knew it was

pointless. Due to a rash of late-night crank calls last month, her parents had started shutting off their ringer when they went to bed.

It looked like she was just going to have to sit tight and wait. The dispatcher had said she'd call for Jenny's exact location as soon as she had a truck available.

Jenny shut off her lights and shrunk down in her seat, praying that anyone driving would think the car was unoccupied. The last thing she wanted was for some stranger to stop.

She wasn't sure how long she'd been sitting there when a familiar melody rose from her purse.

Damn. She'd forgotten to call Robert. He worried about her driving alone at night and had made her promise to call him as soon as she got home.

She flipped the phone open. "Robert, I'm sorry. I—"

"Jasmine. You're breaking up."

Jenny glanced at the readout and her heart sank. *Low battery.* Could her luck get any worse?

"Did you make it home okay?"

For a second she was tempted to tell him yes. After all, she wasn't his responsibility. But then she realized if he didn't come help her, she'd be spending the night in her car. Because by the time Triple A tried to call, her phone would be dead.

"I have a flat tire," she said quickly, trying to ignore the beeping telling her the phone would soon shut off. "I tried to call for emergency road service but they're all—"

"Where are you?" he asked.

She gave him the directions as best she could. "You don't have—"

"I'll be right there." His tone brooked no argument. "Keep your windows up and your doors locked. Don't open them for anyone. Understand?"

Her heart warmed at the concern in his voice.

"I won't." Love for this man welled up from deep inside, making it difficult to speak. "Thank you."

"Doors locked," he repeated, and then he was gone.

Ten minutes later a vehicle slowed and stopped behind her. Icy fingers of fear slithered up her spine. Even if Robert had left immediately, it would have taken him a good twenty minutes to reach her.

Every sordid tale she'd every heard or read of roadside assaults flashed through her mind. She pulled the keys from the ignition, her fingers curving around a tiny vial of pepper spray her father had given her. If they broke in, she'd go down fighting. She heard footsteps but kept her gaze focused straight ahead.

A tapping sounded at the window, and she reluctantly shifted her gaze.

The breath she'd been holding came out in a whoosh of relief.

"Dad." She stuck the key in the ignition, then lowered the window. "What are you doing here?"

"We got your message," he said, "but when we tried to call you back, it went to voice mail."

"My phone's dead." She pushed open the car door and stepped out. "I must have forgotten to charge it last night."

The car door of her parents' Buick opened, then slammed shut.

"Mom came with you?"

"She insisted." Her father's lips curved up in a wry smile. "I told her she didn't have to—but you know your mother."

Carol Carman hurried over, her face filled with concern. "Darling, are you okay? I was so worried . . ."

Her mother wasn't the only one who was worried. Fear knotted Jenny's stomach. She shifted from one foot to the other, resisting the urge to glance at her watch. The way she figured it, she had ten minutes max to get rid of her parents. "I'm sorry you came out for nothing."

Her father's brows pulled together. "What do you mean, for nothing? Looks to me like that tire still needs changing."

"It does. But I was able to reach a friend and he's on his way." Jenny forced a bright smile. "So there's no need for you to stay. You can just head back home—"

"And leave you here? Alone?" The look of shock and disbelief on her mother's face would have been laughable at any other time. "Absolutely not."

"But he's coming," Jenny couldn't keep the desperation from her voice. "There's no need—"

"And what if he can't find you?" her father asked, reminding her of Annie with his chin set in that stubborn tilt. "I agree with your mother. I'll start changing the tire and if your friend shows up he can help."

"Is this your new boyfriend?" Her mother's eyes brightened. "I've been wanting to meet him."

A set of headlights pulled up behind the Buick, and even in the dim light, Jenny recognized Robert's Land Rover.

Her heart plummeted. "Well, it looks like you're going to get your wish."

Seventeen

Robert made the trip that should have taken twenty-five minutes in fifteen, cursing himself for letting Jasmine make the late-night drive alone.

His heart was in his throat the entire way. And when he saw her car with an unfamiliar vehicle parked behind it, he prayed she'd followed his instructions and kept the doors locked.

He was out of his vehicle the minute the Land Rover stopped, his hands clenched into fists.

But he relaxed when he realized the Buick LeSabre belonged to an older couple.

The fact that they would stop on this stretch of roadway to help a stranger surprised him. But he was grateful. At least Jasmine hadn't had to wait alone.

"Robert." Jasmine stepped forward, her face tight with strain.

He moved toward her, wanting nothing more than to hold her in his arms and reassure himself that she was okay. But the older woman stepped between them, thwarting his efforts.

Actually she wasn't as old as he'd first thought. Her face was relatively unlined and her hair was a dark blond, not gray. He decided she was probably in her early fifties. She held out her hand and he shook it automatically, his eyes still on Jasmine.

"I'm Carol Carman, Jenny's mother." She gestured with the other hand to the thin man with glasses now standing beside her. "This is my husband, Lloyd."

Jenny? Jasmine had spoken of her friend Marcee, but he couldn't recall her ever mentioning a *Jenny*.

"Jen told us you were on your way," Lloyd said. "And that we didn't have to wait. But I wasn't about to leave my baby girl out here all alone."

"Of course not," Robert agreed, even as confusion muddled his brain.

Robert shifted his gaze to Jasmine, hoping for some answers. She looked away.

The man held out his hand. "Lloyd Carman."

"Robert Marshall."

"I'm happy we were finally able to meet," Carol said. "We told Jenny to bring you around but she seemed determined to keep you all to herself."

Robert's smile froze on his face. These were . . . Jasmine's parents?

Apparently satisfied that he'd been appropriately cordial, Lloyd returned to business and retrieved the spare from the trunk. Carol handed Robert the lug wrench and he squatted down by the wheel, grateful to have something to do while his mind tried to process this new information.

Perhaps he was jumping to all the wrong conclusions. Maybe there was a logical explanation.

Jasmine bent over and rested a hand on his shoulder, her mouth close to his ear. "I'll explain," she said. "After they leave."

"Did you and Jenny meet at D&D?" Carol asked.

Jasmine's fingers dug into his shoulder.

"D&D?" Robert's hand froze on the wrench.

"Dodson and Dodson. You know, the accounting firm where Jenny works." Carol's voice faltered. "I just assumed you met through her job . . ."

Robert glanced up at Jasmine, not sure

how to respond. An uncomfortable silence descended.

"Robert and I met at O'Malley's," Jasmine said. "It's a sports bar in Lincoln Park. The Cubs were playing at Wrigley."

"And losing, no doubt." Lloyd chuckled, placing the spare on the ground next to Robert.

"Lloyd," Carol said sharply. "The Cubbies don't always lose."

"You like the Cubs, *Jenny*?" Robert gave the wrench a hard jerk, loosening the last bolt. With lips pressed together, he pulled the tire from its mounting.

He turned and met her gaze, willing her to deny the name, to say this was all some sort of sick joke.

Instead she flushed and kicked at the dirt with the toe of her shoe.

"She's a big fan," Carol said.

"He didn't ask you." Lloyd grunted and took the tire—what was left of it, anyway—from Robert.

"I'm surprised you didn't already know that," Carol said.

"Mom," Jenny said. "Stop."

"Stop what?" Carol's tone didn't hold even a hint of apology. "You two have been dating for a while. That's kind of a basic thing."

"You're right," Robert said. Though his words were directed to Carol, his gaze remained riveted on Jenny. "It *is* a basic kind of thing. I guess it makes me wonder what else about your daughter I don't know."

Even in the darkness he could see the stricken look in Jenny's eyes.

Robert turned his attention back to the spare tire Lloyd had placed on the ground next to him. He lifted and shoved it into place, then silently tightened each bolt. He popped the hubcap back on and shifted his gaze back to Jasmine. Or Jenny. Or whoever she was.

"All done," he said.

Jenny watched her parents drive away with a mixture of dread and relief. She and Robert were finally alone. But now that they were, she wasn't sure what to say or where to even start.

All she knew was that the hurt in his eyes tore at her heart, and at the moment she doubted there was anything she could say that could make this horrible situation better. Still, for his sake, she had to try.

"Robert. I—" she began.

"Jenny," he interrupted, not giving her a chance to continue. "That is your name, isn't it? Not Jasmine Coret, but Jenny Carman?"

His words were more accusation than question but he seemed to expect an answer. She hesitated, then nodded.

"Let me take a wild guess. Your parents— Lloyd and Carol—don't live in Arizona and they aren't French. You probably don't even have a sister."

"I do," she said. "Annie. She's seventeen—"

"So *everything* wasn't a lie, just most of it."

"Not most of it," Jenny said. "Just my name and where I work . . . and that stuff about my parents."

She spoke quickly, the words tumbling out one after the other. Maybe if he understood that she'd only lied on those few things it would be okay. Right now she had his full attention and she had to make the most of it. "Everything else was true."

He lifted a brow, and she could see the skepticism in his eyes. "Everything?"

She nodded.

His gaze turned sharp and assessing. "The girl at Navy Pier. Was she really a former neighbor?"

For one crazy second, Jenny was tempted to lie. But the urge passed and she shook her head. "No. But—"

"What about Margaret?" His lips had tightened into a hard, straight line, and her heart fluttered. "She didn't really tell you where I'd be, did she? You were there doing an audit."

Jenny licked her suddenly dry lips. She opened her mouth, then shut it. Why bother? The look in his eyes said he already knew the answer.

"So it wasn't just your name and where you work." His voice held more resignation than anger.

Hope rose in her breast. He hadn't just stormed off. So maybe there still was a chance. "I didn't want to lie to you—"

"Then why did you?" The bite in the words was unmistakable.

"It started out as a joke." Jenny stopped herself, realizing too late that in her nervousness, she was handling this all wrong.

"What we had was a *joke*?"

"No. No." The flutter in her heart turned to a full-fledged quiver. "I never said that."

"Yes. You did." Even in the dim light his eyes were cold as steel. "Do you even listen to what you say?"

"Let me just explain—"

"I think I've heard enough."

Jenny wanted to stomp her foot in frustration. Nothing was coming out right. Despite the coolness in his gaze, she knew she'd hurt him and she desperately wanted to make him understand what they'd shared hadn't been a joke. It had been real.

She grabbed his arm. "You owe it to me to at least listen—"

"I don't owe you anything." His voice was hard. His gaze harder. "And none of this matters anyway because it's over between us."

"Robert." Tears sprang to Jenny's eyes. "Please—"

"Jasmine, let—" He stopped himself and exhaled a ragged breath. "Let it go, *Jenny*. You had your fun, but now it's over. And the joke was on me."

His voice had grown thick and he whirled and headed for the Land Rover. The engine turned over. Without another word, he was gone.

Jenny watched his taillights disappear from view, and by the time she finally spoke, there was no one to hear.

"You're wrong, Robert," she said. "The joke is on me."

Robert pulled back the living room drapes and watched the lights of downtown Chicago blink at him.

How he'd made it through the past week, he wasn't sure. He'd hoped it would get easier, but instead each hour without Jasmine—Jenny, he reminded himself—only got harder.

He missed talking to her, missed teasing her, missed having her in his bed. But most of all he missed *her*.

Her smile.

Her laugh.

Her incredible appetite.

Robert's lips twitched even as his heart twisted. Saturday night and nowhere to go. Before Jasmine, work had consumed his time. He hadn't minded the isolation. But that was before he'd discovered what he'd been missing.

Restless, he crossed the living room and flipped on the television. A sitcom was playing and he left it on, hoping it would improve his mood, but the canned laughter was like nails on a blackboard. He muted the volume and turned to the stereo, wanting something to fill the awful stillness.

Music from the CD, the one that had been playing the last time they'd made love, filled the room. He listened for a few minutes, remembering how soft her skin had been beneath his fingers. How sweet her lips had tasted. How—

Clenching his jaw against the bittersweet memories, Robert turned abruptly and left the room, leaving the love songs playing in the background.

He stood at the kitchen counter for the longest time before grabbing a glass and a bottle of wine. He poured himself some and returned to the living room, taking a seat facing the window.

Memories of her washed over him, gently lapping at his self-control. They'd shared so much in such a short time. Robert took a sip of wine and drew a ragged breath.

All his life he'd hoped that one day he'd find that special someone, the one he'd want beside him forever. He'd been convinced Jasmine was that woman. That she was his . . . soul mate.

His lips tightened. How could she have fooled him so completely? He'd always been a good judge of character. But he hadn't seen through her. And no matter how he tried, he couldn't understand why she'd lied.

Forty-five minutes later, the bottle was almost empty and Robert was still pondering the question. The knock on the door aroused only mild curiosity. But when the light tap turned to pounding, he realized the person wasn't going away.

Holding the bottle in one hand, Robert crossed the room and pulled open the door.

His brother stood in the hallway. Dressed in faded jeans and a T-shirt, Will looked more like the brother of his youth than the CEO of a large corporation.

"Do you have a minute?" Will's gaze dropped to the bottle in Robert's hand. "Unless you have company . . ."

"No company." Robert motioned Will inside with the bottle. "Care to join me? It's a good year . . . I think."

Surprise skittered across Will's face but his expression remained wary. "Sure."

"Have a seat." Robert gestured toward the living room before heading into the kitchen. He poured some wine into a glass, then returned to the living room with the bottle in one hand, Will's glass in the other. "So what brings you by, little brother?"

Will took the glass Robert offered and leaned back in the chair. Though his pose was decidedly casual, the tension in his shoulders gave him away. He didn't answer immediately. Instead his gaze dropped to the briefcase he'd placed next to the chair.

Business must be decidedly worse, Robert surmised, for Will to swallow his pride a second time.

He should just tell him to go home. But the

wine had given Robert a faint buzz, and for some reason he wasn't quite so angry tonight. At least not with Will.

"What's the latest with LDM?" Robert asked in a conversational tone.

Will took a sip of wine. "I thought you weren't interested."

"I'm not," Robert said with a shrug. "Not really."

Even as he said the words, Robert wondered how they'd gotten to this point, so cool and distant. When had they become more like strangers than brothers?

Actually, Robert didn't have to think hard to pinpoint when it had all started. It was when Will had been offered the CEO position. No, that wasn't entirely true, Robert thought. It had started when Will had *accepted* the position without a single word of protest.

To this day, Robert couldn't understand how his brother could have taken something that he knew didn't belong to him.

He'd asked Will that question many times over the past two years but had never gotten a straight answer.

Robert decided it was time to ask again. "Why did you do it, Will?"

An uncertain look furrowed his brother's brow. "Why did I come over? I wanted—"

"I don't care about that." Robert waved a dismissive hand. "Why did you accept the CEO position when you knew it should have been mine?"

"It was Dad's decision—"

"Bullshit." The word shot from Robert's lips. "You could have turned it down."

"I don't want to go back down that road—"

"Well, I do," Robert said. He'd already lost the woman he loved. Maybe he'd end up losing his brother, too. But he wanted answers. He deserved answers. "I have a right to know."

Will rose and moved to the window. He stared into the darkness, the wineglass still in his hand. "I shouldn't have kept this from you."

A sense of unease coursed up Robert's spine. He took another drink. "Tell me."

Will continued to stare out the window. "From the time we were little I knew that one day you would be running LDM. I accepted that fact."

It wasn't Will's words, rather something in his voice that struck an off chord. "You make it sound like you resented me."

"Not when I was small." Will turned to face

Robert. "But in college . . . Of course by then it was you and Dad. I was just the other brother, the third wheel."

A disturbing thought crept into Robert's consciousness. "So you'd been lobbying Dad for the job behind my back? Is that what happened?"

"Of course that's not what happened," Will snapped. "Dad came to *me*. He said he was thinking of retiring and wanted me to take over."

"Just like that." Robert's tone reflected his skepticism. "He offered you the job."

"I was shocked." Will's eyes took on a distant, faraway look. "I was flattered."

"You didn't *wonder* why he chose you over me?" Robert asked. "The thought didn't cross your mind?"

"I'm not stupid, Robert." Will's gaze narrowed. "Of course I asked."

"And?"

"He told me I was the best man for the position."

It was the same old unsatisfying answer Will had always given. Robert leaned back in his seat and drained his glass. "And so you said yes."

A tiny smile—the first of the night—lifted Will's lips. "Actually I turned him down."

"You did what?" Robert straightened in his

chair and set the empty glass on the table. He hadn't heard this before.

"Then I told him that we both knew you were the best man and that the job belonged to you," Will said in a matter-of-fact tone. "Needless to say, he didn't appreciate the input."

"I bet not." Robert could only imagine his father's response. Lawrence Marshall had never liked anyone second-guessing his decisions, not even family.

"Dad said that he'd rather sell out than give you the job. He claimed your judgment was flawed. He was firmly convinced if you took control of LDM, the company would be bankrupt within three years." Will leaned forward. "He said you couldn't be trusted."

There was a long, brittle silence.

Couldn't be trusted? Hot anger rose inside Robert. No wonder Will hadn't wanted to tell him this before. Robert opened his mouth to defend himself, then shut it without a word leaving his lips. It was obvious that Will found him trustworthy. Otherwise he wouldn't have asked for his help.

"He also let me know in no uncertain terms that if I didn't accept the position, he'd give it to Jay Moran," Will added.

For a second Robert was struck speechless.

Jay Moran had headed up their South American division for over ten years. He was a longtime employee, a brilliant businessman, but . . . "Jay isn't family."

"Exactly." Will picked up the bottle and emptied the last of the Merlot into his glass. "I couldn't let that happen. I may not have been as involved with the company as you were, but I cared about it. I wanted LDM to be headed by a Marshall."

"What the hell was he thinking?"

Will swirled the wineglass, and his gaze turned pensive. "I didn't realize until later why he'd really chosen me."

Robert heard the pain in his brother's voice. And, as eager as he was to have all the pieces to this puzzle revealed, he didn't push. He'd waited two years to learn the truth. He could wait a few minutes longer.

"It took a while, but I finally figured it out. Dad didn't choose me because I was the best; he picked me because he wanted to play armchair quarterback." A trace of bitterness underscored Will's revelation. "With me or Jay at the helm—"

"He stayed in control." It suddenly all made sense. Robert had wondered why Will had never made his mark on the company. Why the company had continued to plug along in ultra-conservative mode. Now he knew.

But just because his father wanted to call the plays didn't mean Will had to keep him in the game. According to the company's bylaws, the CEO of LDM had the final say on all decisions concerning the corporation. It was the main reason Robert had looked forward to being promoted. "You've always had the power to take complete charge. You just have to exercise it."

Will rubbed a weary hand over his face. "Sometimes I think it'd be easier just to sell."

Robert made a sound of disgust. "Of course it'd be *easier*. But that doesn't mean it's the *right* course of action. This is our company, Will. One that will be passed down to our children. To Leah and her future brothers and sisters. To my children, should I have any."

An image of a baby with Jasmine's honey blond hair and big blue eyes flashed before him, but he shoved it aside. Jasmine was Jenny, and that dream was as unreal as her name.

"I'm over my head," Will said almost to himself. "Dad shoots down all my suggestions but doesn't come up with anything better. At this point I don't know how I can dig the company out of the hole it's in, even if I wanted to try."

Robert glanced at the briefcase sitting on the

floor. "I assume you brought the financial reports. Why don't we start with the numbers and go from there?"

"I wanted to succeed." Will's shoulders slumped, and he suddenly looked much older than his thirty years. "I wanted so much to be a success, to show you and Dad that I could handle it. But all I've done is single-handedly destroy our family legacy."

The pain in his eyes tore at Robert's heart. He should be elated. This was what he'd thought he'd wanted. But running LDM no longer held the appeal it once did. And neither did seeing his brother fail.

When had his priorities changed?

Since his relationship with Jenny . . .

No, he couldn't give her the credit.

"Let's start with the figures," Robert said. "But first, we need more wine."

It was close to two by the time they finished. It became quickly apparent that Lawrence's strategy had been to focus on what had worked in the past. Not a single one of Will's innovative suggestions had been tried.

But that would soon change, Robert thought with a smile. He and Will had developed a battle plan, a way to save the company. A plan that Will would begin implementing tomorrow.

Time would be a factor, but Robert knew Will would succeed. And when he did, Robert would rejoice along with him.

"Dad's not going to like it," Will said. "You don't drop to second string without a fight."

"He'll adjust," Robert said. "Dad doesn't want the company to fail any more than we do. And, in some ways, being out of the hot seat might be a relief."

"If you'd been in charge, we'd never be at this point."

"Probably not," Robert admitted, seeing no need to sugarcoat the truth. Obviously his father hadn't been ready for retirement, and this had been his way of placating his wife and doctors, while remaining in control.

It was so simple. Robert wondered why it had taken him so long to see it.

Of course, he hadn't been able to see beyond Jasmine's lies, either.

"Women," Robert muttered.

Will tilted his head. "What did you say?"

"Nothing," Robert said. "I was just thinking of something else."

"Or is it some*one* else?" The lines that had furrowed Will's brow earlier had completely disappeared, and his smile turned teasing. "I have to say I was surprised to find you alone tonight. I thought for sure you'd be 'entertaining' again."

Robert's heart clenched.

"I thought she was the one. We—" Robert stopped himself. He hadn't gotten where he was in the business world by dwelling on the past. "We're not together anymore."

"What happened?" Will poured himself another glass of wine and leaned back in the chair, in no apparent hurry for the long cab ride home.

Robert thought about telling his brother it was none of his concern. But to shut Will out now seemed wrong.

"She lied." Robert kept his tone matter-of-fact, not wanting Will to see how much Jenny had hurt him. "About everything."

Will paused, the look in his eyes clearly skeptical. "*Everything* covers a lot of territory. There's only so much a person can fake."

"Not in this case." The look Robert shot Will dared him to disagree.

"Okay, let's suppose she did lie about everything." Will took another sip of wine, surprisingly agreeable. "Why'd she do it?"

Robert steeled his heart against the pain. "She said it was a joke."

Will's brows pulled together in puzzlement.

"That doesn't make sense. What kind of joke?"

"I have no idea." Robert's fingers tightened around the stem of his wineglass. "Once I realized the extent of her lies, I'd heard enough."

"You didn't hear her side?" Will asked. "Weren't you curious?"

"No." Robert spoke through gritted teeth. He hadn't been curious. He'd been angry. Now he just didn't care. "It's over. I just want to forget I ever knew her and move on with my life."

"That isn't always easy to do," Will said. "Especially when emotions are involved."

The sympathy in Will's tone broke the last of Robert's tightly held control.

"So what's your point?" Robert snapped.

"Like you said earlier, just because something is *easier* doesn't mean it's the *right* course of action." Will poured a splash of wine into his glass. He stared down into the burgundy liquid, and for a brief second a hint of sadness stole over his features. "Pretending the problem doesn't exist doesn't solve anything. I learned that the hard way."

Robert's anger dissolved as he realized that Will was speaking from experience.

"Before you can have closure and move on, you have to address the issue," Will added.

"You think I should talk to her?"

"Believe me, I'm the last one who should be giving advice," Will said, meeting his brother's gaze. "But if it means anything, I'm glad *we* talked. I'm only sorry it took so long."

After she treated Annie to lunch, Jenny and her sister went shopping. The two wandered through several small specialty shops before entering the air-conditioned coolness of a large Michigan Avenue department store. Jenny didn't even need to ask her sister where they should go first. Once a serviceable-shoe maven, Jenny now shared Annie's passion for stylish footwear.

Annie immediately zeroed in on a pair of simple woven flats in hot pink. She flipped one over, and her eyes widened.

"A little pricey?"

"If Dad gave me a decent allowance I could buy them," Annie muttered.

Jenny hid a smile. Two-hundred-fifty-dollar Stuart Weitzmans? Her father would have to be paying Annie a *salary* rather than an allowance for her to afford such shoes.

Still, they were cute. Jenny trailed a finger along the side of the pink leather. "I love 'em."

"You should buy them," Annie said promptly. "You make the big bucks."

Jenny's heart clenched—but only for a second. "Not anymore. As of this morning I am o-fficially out of work."

Annie dropped the shoe back on the display with a thud. "Shut up."

Jenny picked up a pair of turquoise beaded flip-flops, surprised at her own casual attitude. "Didn't you wonder why I didn't have to rush back to work after lunch?"

"What happened?"

"Reduction in force," Jenny said simply, opting for the pat explanation she'd been given.

A look of sympathy crossed Annie's face. "What are you going to do?"

"I called my contact at Kyllie's," Jenny said. "They told me I made the final cut. I should know if I have the job by next Wednesday or Thursday."

Managing the accounting department of the popular clothing firm was Jenny's first choice, but she knew better than to count on being the chosen one. On Saturday she'd be sending out more résumés.

"Someone will hire you." Annie nodded her head in extra emphasis. "You're cute. And you have a fabulous fashion sense. You're also smart and great with numbers."

Annie's confidence warmed Jenny's heart. The funny thing was, two months ago she wasn't sure her sister would have felt the same way.

"Thank you, Annie," Jenny said, clearing her throat. "Your support means a lot."

But Annie didn't appear to be listening. Instead her sister's gaze was now focused somewhere behind Jenny's shoulder.

Annie's brows drew together. "Isn't that Robert?"

Jenny's heart slammed against her ribs. She whirled. A second later her breath came out in a whoosh.

The tall, dark-haired man at the tie display was about Robert's age and build, but the similarity ended there. The guy was nowhere near as handsome as Robert.

Robert. God knew she'd never meant to hurt him.

The pain in his eyes still haunted her. She'd tried to explain. But in that moment of extreme stress she'd reverted to a blithering idiot who'd only made things worse with each word.

There was so much she hadn't said on that roadside. So much she still needed to say. That's why she'd cast aside her pride and kept calling. She'd wanted to make sure he understood why she'd lied and that what they'd shared had never been a *joke*.

She shifted her gaze and found Annie staring.

"Is it him?" her sister asked.

Jenny shook her head.

"Have you heard from him lately?"

"He doesn't return my calls," Jenny said simply.

"You don't seem that upset." Annie's gaze turned quizzical. "I thought you really liked him."

There was genuine puzzlement in the girl's voice, and Jenny realized Annie was confusing *coping* with *not caring*. Her sister had no idea what the last couple of weeks had been like for her. How hard it had been for her to wake up every morning knowing the man she loved no longer loved her.

But the past two weeks had also taught Jenny a lot about herself.

" 'In the midst of winter, I finally learned that there was in me an invincible summer,' " Jenny murmured.

"What did you say?" Annie asked.

"I said I don't want to talk about Robert." Jenny softened the words with a slight smile. "It's over. I've accepted that some things are unforgivable."

"You lied about your *name*," Annie said. "Big deal."

"And about where I worked." Jenny lifted a hand and ticked off the fingers. "And about talking to his—"

"You're so dramatic." Annie rolled her eyes. "You didn't kill his mother. Or steal his credit card. Or cheat on him. In the grand scheme of things what you did was definitely *not* unforgivable."

"I lied." A lump formed in Jenny's throat. "Robert didn't deserve that."

Annie stared at her for a long moment. "Yeah," she admitted. "You're right."

Jenny started to say that she had no choice now but to move on, but the words lodged in her throat. She *needed* to move on. One day she would. But right now her heart still belonged to him.

Even if he doesn't want it.

Unwanted tears filled her eyes, but Jenny quickly blinked them back, hoping Annie wouldn't notice.

But her sister's assessing gaze turned sympathetic.

"Don't give up." Annie rested a reassuring hand on her arm. "He won't stay away much longer. He loves you."

Annie sounded so confident, for a second Jenny was tempted to believe her—until her common sense returned. "Where did you ever get such a crazy idea?"

"It's not crazy," Annie said indignantly. "Mom told me that when Robert got out of his car the night you had the flat tire, she could see the lovelight shining in his eyes."

Jenny gave a halfhearted chuckle, wistfully wishing she was still naïve enough to believe in a mother's infallibility.

"It's not funny." Annie's eyes flashed. "Mom knows these things. She knew Tommy and I weren't meant to be together before we knew it ourselves."

Jenny shook her head. "If Robert loved me, he'd return my calls. He'd give me a chance to explain."

"I'm sure he's hurt and confused. And probably thinking if you loved him, you wouldn't have lied," Annie pointed out.

"But I *do* love him." Jenny's voice broke. She shifted her gaze back to the colorful sandals, using the time to regain her composure. "It was a complicated situation. Now we're at a stalemate. I guess that's how it ends."

Jenny expected Annie to argue, to insist that a happy ending *was* in her future. Instead

Annie remained silent, a thoughtful look on her face.

Though Jenny was surprised, she was also relieved. Her sister's response indicated that Annie was beginning to see the light. And Jenny was glad. The sooner both of them accepted the fact that her relationship with Robert was history, the better.

Eighteen

"Who did you say you were?"

The door to the reception area stood slightly ajar and Margaret's imperious tone wafted into Robert's office.

"I'm his sister, Annie," a confident but young female answered. "And I'd prefer you didn't announce me. I'd like to surprise him."

"I'm sure you would surprise him," Margaret answered, and Robert swore he heard a hint of amusement in her voice. "Considering Mr. Marshall only has one sibling, a brother."

"That you know of," the girl retorted.

Now he was intrigued. Obviously his "sister" wasn't the least bit intimidated by Margaret. Robert shoved back his chair, rose to his feet, and headed to the outer office area.

The young woman had her hands on her

hips. "He'll be angry if he finds out I was here and you—"

She stopped as the door swung fully open and Robert stepped out. He paused and stared at Annie. Though she wore a brightly colored dress instead of shorts and a T-shirt, it took only a second for Robert to make the connection. She was the girl from the Pier. The one who'd been talking to Jas—Jenny. "What are you doing here?"

"Surprise." From the girl's reaction, you'd have thought they *were* brother and sister. She smiled broadly, slipped around Margaret, and gave him a hug. "I come bearing news."

Robert stiffened and took a step back, trying to figure out what was going on. His jaw clenched. Jenny must have sent her. But why now?

He lifted a brow. "News?"

"About a mutual acquaintance," the girl added.

Annoyance mingled with amusement. Robert studied the brazen teenager, tempted to send her on her way. But she'd piqued his curiosity, and he couldn't help but wonder what she'd come to say.

What the hell . . .

He gestured with one hand toward his office. "I've got a few minutes."

Shooting Margaret a triumphant look, the girl sashayed into his office, head held high.

Robert ignored Margaret's questioning look and shut the door behind him.

Annie stood in the center of the large office, surveying the opulent surroundings with unabashed interest.

He touched the back of a burgundy chair, and once she'd plopped herself down, he rounded the desk and sat down.

She smiled brightly but didn't say a word.

His respect for her inched up a notch. It was amazing that one so young had already learned that silence was power. He bowed to the inevitable and spoke first. "Mind telling me what this is all about?"

Her lips turned up in a slight smile. "You remember me, huh?"

"You were at the Pier." He struggled to remember. "Former neighbor?"

"Current sister." The girl held out her hand. "Annie Carman."

Robert shook it and his heart clenched. He must have been blind not to see the resemblance. Same honey blond hair. Same blue eyes. Same determined demeanor. He'd almost convinced himself he was over Jenny, but seeing this younger version of her made him realize how far he still had to go. "Why are you here?"

Her eyes widened at his abrupt tone, but her composure didn't waver. "Do you love my sister?"

The bluntness of the question took Robert by surprise. He wasn't sure why, since it was just what he would have expected from Jasmine, er, Jenny. Still, he wasn't about to air his feelings to this stranger. "What kind of question is that?"

His tone left no doubt how he felt about her intrusion into his privacy, but she didn't so much as bat an eye. Instead she met his steely gaze with one of her own. "Do you?"

"I don't know her." Robert shoved back his chair and rose to his feet. All the feelings he'd tried so hard to suppress—love, anger, hurt, bitterness—rose like bile inside him. "She's a liar. I don't know what's true and what's not."

"I don't know what she told you," Annie said. "Or even why she lied. I only know she's miserable."

Good, Robert almost said. At least he wasn't alone in his misery. It wasn't a very charitable thought, but then he wasn't feeling particularly charitable at the moment.

"She won't be miserable for long," he said instead. "I'm sure she'll be out partying with her friends in no time."

His heart twisted at the image of her laughing on the Ferris wheel, cotton candy on her lips. No, it wouldn't be long before she had another guy on her arm. A woman like Jenny wouldn't stay lonely.

"Partying? Out with friends?" Annie started to laugh, then stopped as if realizing she'd been too quick with her initial response. "Maybe. But you'd never have seen that a few months ago."

"What do you mean?"

"She was the ultimate in boring," Annie said. "Big nerd."

"I don't believe it," Robert said, feeling an absurd need to defend Jenny.

"She'd go to Laundryland on Friday nights." Annie's nose wrinkled.

Annie looked so distressed, Robert couldn't help but smile. He quickly sobered, reminding himself who it was they were talking about. "That doesn't sound like the Jenny I knew."

"That's what I'm trying to tell you," Annie said. "My sister has changed since she met you. She doesn't talk about boring accounting problems all the time. She dresses in cool clothes.

And, well, she smiles a lot. Or at least she did . . . before, you know . . . before the two of you broke up."

Robert's fingers tightened around a pencil. "Lots of people smile a lot."

"Not my sister," Annie said. "Before she met you she was super serious, no fun at all. When she got nice things she'd squirrel them away, waiting for some special day."

A sudden image of Jenny with the moonstone flashed before him. Her puzzling words finally made sense.

"Big nerd," Annie repeated, nodding her head for emphasis.

Robert stayed silent. He couldn't make himself agree. "What's your point?"

"Don't get me wrong. My sister may have her faults, but she's a good person," Annie said. "I hate seeing her so sad. Maybe if you talked to her, you two could—"

"Kiss and make up?"

The heavy dose of sarcasm in his voice made her wince. But she immediately rallied and lifted her chin. "Why not? People do it all the time. It's practically a national pastime."

Robert had the almost overwhelming urge to snap at her. To remind her that forgiving and forgetting was for minor relationship infractions, not for major deceptions. But he never got the chance.

Annie glanced at the clock. Her eyes widened. "Is that the right time?"

Robert nodded.

"Yikes." She jumped up and hurried across the thick carpet as fast as her flip-flops would allow. "I'm going to be late for my pedicure."

Annie stopped at the door and turned, one hand resting on the knob, apparently deciding there was time for one last comment. "Call her. Dr. Phil says if you love someone and you have a problem, nothing gets resolved unless you talk."

The girl was halfway out the door before Robert realized that this time she really meant to leave.

"Wait."

She whirled around.

"What makes you think I love her?"

Annie shot him a saucy wink. "If you didn't, you'd have let that she-creature at the reception desk send me away."

Her smile reminded him so much of Jenny that for a second Robert swore she was standing in front of him. And, dear God, he found himself wishing it were as simple as Annie made it seem.

"You think you've got all the answers,"

Robert said, a trifle harshly. "It's not always that easy."

"All I'm asking is that you talk to her," Annie said. "I can't have a sister doing laundry on Friday nights. I have an image to uphold."

Annie had barely left when Bill James stuck his head inside the door. "I told Margaret I'd announce myself. We *were* meeting at five, right?"

Robert glanced at the clock and suppressed a groan. While he was being told off by a seventeen-year-old, his soon-to-be business partner had been left cooling his heels in his waiting room.

"I apologize." Robert moved to shake Bill's hand, then gestured to a chair. "If this happens again tell Margaret she has my permission to interrupt. You shouldn't have to wait."

"I appreciate that." Bill settled into the chair in front of Robert's desk. "I'm afraid we're going to have to keep this short. It's my anniversary and I promised my wife I'd be home early."

Somehow Robert managed to keep the smile on his face. Not long ago he'd been looking forward to having a wife of his own. "Have you been married long?"

"Twenty years too long," Bill said, and then he laughed. "Actually they've been good years. Not to say we haven't had some rough patches."

His candor surprised Robert. "Did you ever think about calling it quits?"

"Stella's made me plenty angry," Bill said with a rueful smile. "But I can't imagine spending my life with anyone but her. She's everything I ever wanted."

"You're a lucky man." Fighting back a rush of envy, Robert picked up a report from his desk and redirected the conversation back to the business at hand. It seemed as if they'd barely gotten started when Bill left.

But that was okay with Robert. Though he should have been focusing, he'd found it difficult to concentrate.

She's everything I ever wanted.

The phrase kept running through his head. That's how he'd once felt about Jasmine.

Though he'd promised he wouldn't torture himself anymore, Robert pulled his cell phone from his coat pocket and placed it on the desk in front of him. He punched a few keys, and the sound of Jenny's voice filled the room.

He'd saved all her messages. At the time, he'd told himself it was because he liked to hear the despair in her voice and know he wasn't the only one suffering.

But that was a lie. The distress in her voice stabbed like a knife. Each time he listened he was reminded of how much he loved her. How much he missed her.

Robert flipped the phone shut and leaned back in his chair. From the moment he'd spotted her at O'Malley's, he'd known she was something special.

His lips curved up in a smile, remembering the determined look in her eyes when she'd invited herself up to his place. Once there she'd turned shy . . . but that hadn't lasted long. Her capacity for pleasure had awed and inspired him.

Memories of the times they'd shared came into vivid focus; grinding on the dance floor, talking deferred compensation over ice cream, walking hand-in-hand at Navy Pier.

He'd been convinced she was everything he'd ever wanted. She challenged him with her intellect, humbled him by her caring, and inspired him with her passion.

Robert raked his fingers through his hair and blew out a frustrated breath. Why had she lied? And continued to lie?

He'd thought he didn't need to know, had been convinced the reason didn't matter. But who was he kidding? It was time he quit speculating and picked up the phone and called her.

Maybe she could help him understand.

And if he could understand, maybe he could forgive.

When Jenny had dropped Annie off after an afternoon of power shopping, she'd felt strong and in control. The downward spiral had started when she'd stopped to pick up a few things at the grocery store. She hadn't really thought much about the strawberries she'd put in her cart . . . until she passed the whipped cream.

Though in the past two weeks Robert had never been far from her thoughts, he'd been front and center from that moment on.

Shutting the door of her apartment with her foot, Jenny crossed the living room, a bag of groceries in each arm.

Once in the kitchen, she tried to keep busy, unpacking the groceries, replenishing the refrigerator, and arranging a bouquet of fresh flowers in her grandmother's cranberry vase.

But no matter how busy her hands were, no matter how much she tried to concentrate on cottage cheese, grape juice, and whole wheat bread, her thoughts kept returning to Robert.

Even when she'd been with Annie, she hadn't

been completely successful in banishing him from her mind. When they'd stopped in the lingerie department, Jenny couldn't help but remember the heat in his gaze when he'd first seen her sexy undies. Of course, that was nothing compared to the fire that had burned red-hot when the lingerie had come off.

Jenny exhaled a heartfelt sigh. While she'd thoroughly enjoyed their lovemaking, the loss of sex wasn't what she regretted the most. She missed simply being with him, talking, laughing, or just sitting in comfortable silence. She'd never connected so fully with any man.

Whenever she talked, she had his full attention. It was as if what she had to say was the most important thing in the world, and he didn't want to miss a word of it. He'd never appeared threatened when her opinions differed from his own. Instead his thoughtful questions showed he valued her input.

From that first night, there had been something about Robert that spoke to her. When she was with him, she felt strong and empowered. It was his acceptance of her bold actions that had allowed the Jasmine part of her personality to take hold and thrive.

If not for him, she'd still be living life in gray

scale. Now her eyes had been opened to a big, bright, colorful world.

He'd given so much, yet gotten so little. Not only had he discovered the woman he'd been intimate with had lied about practically everything, she'd told him what they'd shared had been a joke.

A hard lump formed in the pit of her stomach. While she knew guys weren't as sensitive as women, the comment had to have hurt. The devastated look in his eyes still haunted her.

Tears once again threatened, but Jenny stubbornly blinked them back. She was through crying. Tears didn't help, didn't change anything. They needed to talk. She needed to explain.

But she'd screwed up the explanation once. Would another conversation only make things worse? And how could she talk to him when he wouldn't even return her calls?

Jenny's gaze settled on the cranberry glass. For a second it was almost as if her grandmother was there beside her once again, whispering in her ear, telling her that the past didn't determine the future.

Just because she'd botched an explanation once didn't mean she'd blow it a second time. Robert deserved the truth. All of it. And she was going to give it to him, even if she had to tie him down and force him to listen.

Last time she'd been trying to explain as a way to save herself. This time she'd be doing it for the right reason. She'd be doing it for him.

And this time she'd get it right.

Nineteen

The secretary who ushered Jenny into Robert's office reminded her of a drill sergeant; crisp conversation and a take-no-prisoners attitude. But Jenny didn't care. She wasn't interested in participating in meaningless small talk. She was just happy the woman had done as she'd asked.

Jenny wiped suddenly sweaty palms against her skirt and followed the gray-haired secretary into the executive suite.

Robert's back was to her as she entered the room.

"Mr. Marshall," Margaret began.

Robert swiveled in the chair. "I thought I told you I wasn't to be disturbed—"

His gaze settled on Jenny and his words stopped mid-sentence.

Jenny lifted her chin. "Hello, Robert."

The woman beside her stiffened. "I'm sorry, sir. She threatened to—"

"I told her if she didn't let me see you, I'd start screaming." Margaret might be a tad over-zealous but the last thing Jenny wanted was to get the woman in trouble with her boss. "And I wouldn't stop until I saw you. I meant it, too."

An emotion she couldn't identify flared in his eyes, and her heart skipped a beat. It almost looked like a welcome, but maybe he was just relieved she wasn't screaming. At least he hadn't ordered her out of his office. Not yet, anyway.

She watched as he pushed back his chair and stood.

Jenny drank him in; dark business suit, crisp white shirt, short thick hair, and clear blue eyes. God, how she'd missed him.

"We need to talk." She figured she might as well get to the point since he could kick her out at any moment.

"I agree," he said simply.

Jenny widened her eyes. "You do?"

He nodded. "In fact, I was about to call you."

Though he hadn't said a word to his secretary, the woman slipped back and exited the room, pulling the door shut behind her.

Jenny shifted uneasily from one foot to the

other, not quite sure what to make of his mood. He no longer seemed angry. She wasn't sure if that was good or bad.

Still, she decided to capitalize on the possibility he was softening toward her. She took a step closer and lowered her voice to a confidential whisper.

"Let me tell you a little secret," she said, casting a pointed glance at the desk phone. "It doesn't work unless you pick it up and dial."

The words might be similar to ones once uttered by Jasmine. But Jenny no longer had to pretend to be someone else. She'd grown exceedingly comfortable in her new skin. Both the words and the flippant tone were pure Jenny.

Something flickered in the back of Robert's eyes. He turned his hand to reveal a small phone cupped in his palm. "Your number is on the readout."

Her heart fluttered in her chest. She couldn't see the numbers from where she stood, but why would he lie?

"Why were you calling?" she asked.

"Same reason you're here," he said. "We need to talk."

Jenny couldn't hide her surprise. She'd expected him to be resistant, maybe even to throw her out of his office. Only in her dreams had he acquiesced so easily. Of course, in her dreams he'd also pulled her to him and kissed her passionately.

She glanced at his lips and heaved a regretful sigh. But, she reminded herself, this wasn't about her unmet needs; it was about Robert and making it right with him.

"Have a seat." He gestured to a chair in front of his desk, then resumed his own seat.

He folded his hands on the desk, his expression serious. "There's something I want to say to you."

Jenny fought the panic welling up inside her. The last thing she'd expected was for him to have his own agenda. While she realized he had a right to blast her for what she'd done, he simply couldn't go first. If he did, things might escalate, and she might never get a chance to say what was on her mind and in her heart.

"You'll have your chance," Jenny said firmly. "But I go first."

To her surprise, his lips twitched. "Feeling kind of bossy today?"

"Determined," Jenny said. "There's a lot I need to tell you."

The teasing glint that she'd sworn she'd seen in his eyes was gone. His gaze turned watchful. "Fire away."

"How's your brother?"

The question seemed to catch him off-guard. "Will?"

"Last I knew you only had one," Jenny quipped, though the slight tremble in her voice was at odds with her teasing tone.

"Is that why you came by?" Robert's brows pulled together. "To talk about Will?"

Jenny leaned forward and rested her hands on the edge of the desk. "I led you to believe that I thought it was okay for you not to help him. But the fact is I don't think it's okay. He's your brother. You love him. I know you do. And I'm sure he loves you. You two should be able—"

Jenny paused to take a breath and discovered Robert smiling. Her lips tightened. "This is serious."

"I realize that—"

"I don't think you do." Jenny took a deep breath and prayed her words would convince him to at least *consider* helping his brother. "My sister and I worked through our differences. I want the same for you and Will. I realize he hurt—"

"Jenny." Robert lifted his hand. "Will came over. We talked. The company is okay. We're okay."

For a moment Jenny could only stare. Then her heart swelled with pride. Despite everything that had happened between him and his family, Robert had stepped up to the plate and done the honorable thing. "You saved LDM."

"Will did," Robert said. "All I did was assure him he was headed in the right direction."

Something told Jenny that wasn't the whole story. "So will you be running LDM now?"

Robert shook his head. "Will has a good handle on things. He likes what he's doing. And I like the fact that I'm building my own legacy."

He made it sound so easy, so matter-of-fact. But Jenny knew how much being the CEO of LDM had meant to Robert. The fact that he could so graciously give up his birthright to his brother said a lot about his ability to forgive and forget.

If only he could be so forgiving with me . . .

"Is that the only reason you came?" His eyes were hooded, his expression unreadable. "To make sure things were okay between Will and me?"

Maybe it was Robert's closeness. Or the familiar scent of his cologne. Whatever the reason, Jenny found herself feeling strangely off balance.

"Partially," she finally stammered. "But I also came to explain why I lied. I know you said you didn't care but it's important to me that you know the whole story."

She held her breath, not sure how he would respond. His gaze searched her face, looking for—what? She wasn't sure.

"I should have let you explain," he said almost to himself. "I should have listened."

"It was probably for the best," she said. "I wasn't very coherent that night."

He studied her for a long moment, his expression giving nothing away. "Are you feeling coherent now?"

"I am." Jenny brushed a piece of lint from her skirt. This was her opportunity. But now that the time had come, she found herself tongue-tied. "I don't know where to begin."

He smiled encouragingly. "Why don't you start with the night we met?"

Jenny took a deep, steadying breath, moistened her dry lips with her tongue, and forced her thoughts back to that fateful evening.

"The night I went to O'Malley's was a low point for me." Considering the way her insides were shaking, Jenny's voice came out remarkably steady. "My grandmother, whom I dearly loved, had died a few months earlier, and that day I'd been passed over for a promotion at work."

Robert's gaze remained fixed on her with an intensity that made Jenny squirm.

Fighting to hold on to her composure, she forced a nonchalant tone. "Gram had a tendency to focus on the future at the expense of the present. I realized I'd done the same thing. I'd focused so much on my career that I had no life. None. Nada. Zip."

Her fingers rose to her neck and slid over the smooth stone dangling from a silver chain. The moonstone Robert had given her served as a constant reminder of the need for balance in her life. Never again would she let career take precedence over family and friends.

Robert didn't even blink. His only reaction was to steeple his fingers beneath his chin.

Jenny swallowed with difficulty and found her voice again. "I'd gone to the bar determined to have fun. But between you and me I didn't hold out much hope. I'm not good around men. Especially when I get rattled."

Like I am now.

Her body thrummed with nervous tension, and beads of perspiration dotted her brow. She'd hoped he'd give her some indication what he was thinking or maybe toss her another encouraging smile, but he merely continued to stare.

The silence grew deafening. But, she reminded herself, at least she had his full attention.

"To make things even worse, that night Marcee kept insisting I was sexually frustrated and needed to get laid," she blurted out.

His eyes widened in surprise.

Realizing how it must have sounded, Jenny scrambled to clarify. "Of course, jumping into bed with some stranger was the furthest thing from my mind. Heck, I'd gone six years without it. What was the rush?"

The dimple in his cheek flashed and his expression softened. His cough sounded suspiciously like a chuckle.

It was as close to an opening as she was going to get, and she took it. "When I saw you . . . when our eyes met . . ." She paused, fighting the pull of the memory, but in the end she gave in and allowed herself to be swept away. "There was this connection. Like we were on the same wavelength. I had the feeling that even though we didn't know each other, somehow you understood my loneliness. And I understood yours. It was like a scene from a movie. My heart started racing. I couldn't breathe. I went all tingly inside—"

His eyes took on a gleam—or maybe it was a glaze—but she pressed onward. She couldn't stop now. "I wanted to talk to you in the worst way but I was scared. Scared I'd say a couple of words and you'd know I wasn't fun or exciting enough for you."

She closed her eyes briefly, recalling the fear that had gripped her. "Then Marcee left. Shortly after that I saw your friend head out the door, and I knew my chance had come. I told myself that if I pretended to be someone who was confident, I'd be more confident."

Her actions had seemed so reasonable at the time. Now, hearing the echo of her own words in the quiet office, she wasn't so sure.

"So you planned to lie from the very beginning." Disappointment hung heavy in his voice.

"No." Jenny shook her head vigorously. "I only intended to use my grandmother's friend, Jasmine, for *internal* inspiration."

"Jasmine Coret is your grandmother's friend?" His voice rose in disbelief.

"She was," Jenny said. "Jasmine died many years ago—when she was about my age. But according to Gram, she packed more living into those thirty years than most people do in a lifetime."

Robert raised a hand to his head. "I cannot believe you resurrected a dead person."

"Stated like that, it does sound a bit bizarre," Jenny conceded.

Robert's mouth curved in something that was almost—not quite, but almost—a smile, and Jenny's eyes shifted almost compulsively to his.

She suddenly found the words pouring out of her. "I'm so sorry, Robert. I don't really know why I did what I did that night." Without thinking, she reached out, and her breath caught on something that was nearly a sob when he took her hand for the briefest of moments. "When you asked my name, hers just came out. And a hairstylist seemed a much more exciting occupation than a CPA. I'm not sure why I said my father was French or that he lived in Phoenix."

Once she'd started, the tangled explanation kept pouring out. "It seemed so harmless. After all, I was convinced we'd just talk that night and never see each other again."

"But we did," he said, taking advantage of the momentary pause when she drew a breath. "And you continued to let me think you were Jasmine."

"There were so many times I wanted to tell you who I really was, so many times I *planned* to tell you . . . like that last night we were together. I tried. I really did. But the moment wasn't right. And I was . . . afraid."

"Afraid?"

"Of losing you. Of losing Jasmine. Of you finding out just how boring I really am." Jenny pulled her hands into her lap and clasped them together to still their trembling. "I'd never been so happy."

Robert didn't respond immediately and his inscrutable expression gave nothing away. She couldn't tell if hearing the whole unvarnished truth had made him feel better or not. Or if it had changed his opinion of her.

"One thing still isn't clear," he said. "What did you mean when you said that it was all a joke?"

"Like I told you, when I get nervous, things come out wrong. I was referring to the whole name thing." Jenny's gaze turned pleading. "Please believe me. Being with you wasn't a joke. You allowed me to be the person I was meant to be. You are . . . you were . . . the best thing that ever happened to me."

Was it only her imagination or was there a slight softening in the set of his jaw?

"I never meant to hurt you." Though she'd promised herself she wouldn't cry, a tear slipped down her cheek.

"Jenny, don't—" Robert reached out, then stopped himself.

"It might be too late for us, Robert." Jenny's chest tightened, and she could barely get the words past the lump in her throat. "But I want you to know that I never lied to you about my feelings."

"I know that." He stared at her for a long moment, and his gaze turned thoughtful. Only when the clock on the wall began to chime did he rouse and rise to his feet.

Was this it? Was this the end? A frisson of fear shot up her spine. Her heart gave a sickening lurch.

Jenny scrambled to her feet, her breath coming in short puffs, frantic tears pushing at her lids. "Don't hate me, Robert. I couldn't bear to have you hate me."

"You know me better than that," he said, his eyes clear and very, very blue. "I could never hate you."

The words had barely left his mouth when the office door swung open.

Jenny quickly blotted her eyes with the tissue, drew a shaky breath, and turned.

"I'm sorry to disturb you, but Mr. James has arrived and he indicated I was to let you know, even if you were occupied." The secretary's gaze settled momentarily on Jenny before returning to Robert. "Shall I show him in?"

Jenny shifted her gaze to Robert. Indecision flickered in his eyes, but before he had a chance to answer, Bill James appeared in the doorway.

Robert's lips curved up and he rounded the desk. "Bill." He extended his hand. "Good to see you again."

The man took Robert's hand but his gaze slid to Jenny. Recognition flashed in his eyes. "I remember you. Jasmine, right?"

Jenny stood. "Close," she said, her voice remarkably steady. "It's actually Jenny. Jenny Carman."

"I've never been that good with names." Bill gave a self-deprecating chuckle. "But I never forget a pretty face."

Before the words had even left his mouth, Bill turned to Robert. "It's good we're meeting today. I was going through the agreement one last time and there—"

Feeling like she'd already been dismissed, Jenny leaned over and scooped up her bag. "If you'll both excuse me, I must be going."

A few steps and she stood at the doorway. "Good-bye, Robert. Thanks for your time."

Despite knowing it was over, Jenny was tempted to linger, to see if—what? If Robert would blow off an important business meeting for *her*? She knew what growing his empire meant to him. Hadn't he made it clear that first night they were together that work was his priority?

Besides, what really was left to talk about? She'd said everything she wanted to say, explained everything she wanted to explain.

And there really was nothing new he could say to her. She already knew how disappointed he was in her and how much she'd hurt him.

"Thank you," Jenny said in a low tone to Margaret as she slipped past the woman. While she may have threatened to scream, she had the feeling Margaret had seen right through the ploy. Yet the secretary had helped her anyway.

Jenny was rewarded with a sympathetic smile.

Hot tears pushed at the backs of Jenny's lids. She wasn't sure she'd be able to keep them at bay, but somehow she made it to the corridor outside the executive suites without shedding a tear.

At least it was over. She'd owned up to her mistakes and made no excuses. While confessing all her sins to Robert's face hadn't been easy, it had been the right thing to do. And he'd been a true gentleman.

He'd listened to what she'd had to say with few interruptions. Her fear that she'd further added to the estrangement between him and Will had been eased. Even the dreaded secretary had been accommodating.

The visit couldn't have gone better. So why did she feel as if the light had gone out of her world?

Because you love him, a tiny voice inside her head whispered, *and you're enough of a romantic to have hoped for a different outcome.* Unfortunately his response had made it clear that there wasn't going to be any happily-ever-after.

Jenny exhaled a ragged breath.

What had Gram always said—be careful what you wish for?

Well, she'd wanted closure. And it looked like she'd gotten it.

Twenty

Robert watched in disbelief as Jenny walked out of his office. His heart gave a lurch.

Bill continued to babble about some changes that absolutely had to be made today but Robert paid no attention. All he could think about was Jenny.

He hadn't been lying when he'd said he'd been about to call her. But now he was glad that she'd made the first move. After listening to her story, he realized coming to him in this way had been a huge step for her. And even though she'd gone into far more detail with her explanation than necessary, he'd let her talk. She'd seemed so determined to not leave anything out.

The more she'd talked, the more the puzzle pieces had fallen into place. It was unbelievable that she'd resurrected a dead woman on a whim, but he could see how it could have happened. And she'd been right about the loneliness and the instant connection that first night.

If she hadn't been bold and come over to his table, would he have approached her? Probably not.

In a way it was as if the lie had brought them together.

And now it was keeping them apart.

Robert set his jaw. He loved the woman who'd just walked out his door. It didn't matter whether she called herself Jasmine or Jenny or . . . Josephine JuJu, she was the one he wanted with him forever.

"Bill." Robert interrupted the man and called Margaret back into the room. "I have to leave. Margaret can take down your concerns. We'll get back to you."

Robert didn't wait for Bill's response. Frankly, what the other man thought didn't matter. Robert was going after the woman he loved.

And no one was going to get in his way.

Jenny stared down the long hall. While trudging down thirty-two flights held little appeal, it was better than waiting for an elevator and trying to maintain her composure around a bunch of men dressed in three-piece suits.

She'd just spotted the door to the stairs when she was grabbed from behind and spun around.

Jenny opened her mouth to scream but gasped instead when she caught sight of her assailant. "Robert. What are you doing?"

"What does it look like?" he said. "I'm stopping you from leaving me."

Jenny stared into the glittering blue eyes, her heart pounding like a bass drum. "I thought we were finished."

"Not by a long shot," he said softly.

"What about Mr. James?" Jenny asked.

Robert waved a dismissive hand. "Margaret can handle him."

"But we're talking about your business," Jenny said. "It's your priority—"

"*You* are my priority," he said. "Getting things right between us is my—"

"Mr. Marshall." A tall, thin man with a worried frown stopped beside them. "I don't mean to interrupt—"

"Then don't," Robert snapped. His eyes remained focused on Jenny and he didn't even glance in the guy's direction.

Without another word, the man spun on his heel and headed down the hall at a pace that would have done an Olympic speed walker proud.

"I want—" This time Robert's words were interrupted by the ring of his cell phone. He slid his hand into his pocket and silenced it without even looking at the readout. "What I'm trying to say is—"

Raucous laughter sounded from the distance. A noisy group of six or seven women rounded the corner.

Robert swore under his breath. Casting a quick look around, he pulled out a keycard and flashed it in front of a wall-mounted card reader.

There was an audible click, and when Robert pushed down on the handle, the door opened.

"We can talk in here." Robert placed his hand behind her back, urging her forward. "Rod is on vacation."

The lights in the office automatically turned on, and once they were both inside, Robert pulled the door shut and flipped the deadbolt.

Jenny raised a questioning brow.

"I'm not the only one whose card opens all the offices," he explained. "I've a lot to say and I will not be interrupted again."

Jenny hid a smile. She wouldn't want to be the employee who tried to come through that door.

She glanced around. The office was small, with barely enough room for a desk, two chairs, and a credenza. Simple and elegant, but austere.

Other than the computer and phone, the desk surface was completely clear. "Are you sure this Rod guy is coming back? Looks to me like he's moved out."

"He'll be back." Keeping his gaze firmly fixed on her, Robert moved forward until he stood so close, she could feel the heat from his body. "Your sister came to see me."

Jenny desperately wanted to get some distance from the energy that seemed to be coming off him in waves, but she wasn't sure her feet would move, so she stayed where she was, her head spinning. "Annie?"

"Last I knew you only had one," Robert said, mimicking her earlier words. "In case you're worried, she had only good things to say."

Jenny's fingers itched to wrap themselves around Annie's scrawny neck. "I'm sorry she bothered you. She shouldn't have—"

"It's okay," Robert said with a reassuring smile. "We had a nice talk. I like her. She reminds me of you."

Jenny felt an instant's squeezing hurt. If she'd met Robert in another way, in another time, things might have turned out so differently . . .

"Can we talk?" Robert gestured to the two chairs positioned in front of the desk. "I have so much to say."

The fact that he'd asked, rather than ordered, made her decision easy. There was no way she could refuse him.

They both sat down, and after several interminable seconds of silence, Robert began filling her in on his life since she'd last seen him. Once he started speaking, the words tumbled out one after another, and if it were anyone else but Robert, she'd have labeled the discourse pure nervous chatter.

As it was, Jenny found herself listening with only half an ear as her traitorous body responded to his closeness. His deep, masculine rumble sent shivers up her spine. The subtle scent of his cologne brought back erotic memories.

Though she couldn't stop herself from being physically aware of him, Jenny told herself she'd made progress. At least she wasn't weeping on her knees in front of him. And while she might still be madly in love with him, she realized there was no future in loving someone who didn't love her back.

Her mother might still insist she'd seen L-O-V-E in Robert's eyes, but Jenny knew differently. He might have liked her company, might have enjoyed the sex, but that didn't mean he loved her.

". . . a partner."

Jenny jerked back from her reverie and realized with a stab of panic that while she'd been engaged in an internal love-me, love-me-not daisy pull, Robert must have started talking about the new company he was acquiring. And she hadn't even been listening . . .

"You're perfect."

"For what?"

"I'm looking for a partner," he said. "I can't imagine anyone but you in that position."

Robert wanted her to go into business with him? He had to be kidding. But he didn't look as if he was kidding. His eyes were still, watchful, and she felt her heart stutter in her chest.

"That's impossible," Jenny said.

"The job is quite demanding," Robert continued as if she hadn't even spoken. "But you could do it. If you wanted to, that is."

Even if Jenny could get in on this venture with minimal financial investment, she knew "demanding" usually equated to a personal life turned upside down.

And that wouldn't be the only downside. A month ago working closely with Robert would have been a dream come true. Now being near him every day but unable to touch him would be pure torture. And she could only imagine what would happen when one day he found a new love . . . Her heart gave a little ping.

"While I appreciate the vote of confidence . . ." She paused, and her fingers rose to the stone at her neck. "I'm not interested in eighty-hour work weeks."

"You haven't heard the specifics—"

"I don't need to," Jenny said. "No amount of money would be enough to—"

"What about love?" he asked, his voice low and slightly tremulous. "Would that make a difference?"

Jenny blinked in confusion. "I'm not following—"

"I'm talking about you and me." His earnest eyes sought hers. "Partners. Together. Forever."

Her heart slammed against her rib cage with a mighty thud. She lifted a trembling hand to her head, feeling almost dizzy. "You're joking, right?"

"You know me better than that." The beginnings of a smile tipped the corners of his mouth. "The last time we were together you said you loved me. I'm hoping that's still true."

In the time it took her heart to skip a few beats, Robert rose to his feet and took her hand, pulling her to him. He stood so close, she could see the gold flecks in his eyes.

"You're the most incredible woman I've ever known," he said softly. "The past few weeks without you have been pure torture."

Jenny blinked twice, certain this was a dream and she would wake up and find herself alone. But he remained standing in front of her, blue eyes watching her intently.

"What about Jasmine?" she asked. "What about the lies?"

"I don't care what you call yourself. Or what you do for a living. You're the woman I fell in love with, the one I love now, the one I want to be with forever." He cupped her face in his hands. "Jennifer Carman, will you do me the honor of becoming my wife?"

For a second, Jenny swore she could hear the mom-o-meter ringing like crazy in the background. The clanging sounded suspiciously like *I told you so.*

Her heart added to the clatter, beating so hard she could hear the thump in her ears. All the while, the words of love he'd spoken hung in the air between them.

Though Robert's gaze was steady, the hint of uncertainty in his eyes told her that he was nowhere near as confident as he appeared.

"Jenny?"

It was decision time.

Could she live happily ever after with a man who made her laugh with pleasure one minute and moan with desire the next?

A man who accepted her as she was, yet encouraged her to boldly go beyond her comfort zone?

A man who enthusiastically fulfilled her fantasies while at the time inspiring new ones?

Jenny smiled. The answer was so obvious, she didn't need a calculator to know everything added up.

Wrapping her arms around his neck, Jenny plopped a big kiss on his lips, happiness bubbling up inside her. "Yes. Yes. Yes."

She laughed out loud with the sheer joy of it all, and he laughed along with her.

But when he pulled her tight, the laughter died in her throat. Looking up at him in the fluorescent light, she saw his eyes, deep blue and filled with need. Need for her, she realized, feeling a quick flutter of feminine power.

"Remember when you told me that you never mixed business with pleasure?" Her gaze drifted to linger on the desk. She leaned over and ran her hand across the smooth surface. "Well, now that I'm going to be your partner—"

"Wife," he said.

"Wife." She repeated the word, liking the feel

of it on her tongue. "Well, as you know, desktop sex has always been a fantasy of mine, so I was wondering . . ."

The dimple in Robert's cheek flashed. "Tell me you didn't agree to marry me just so you could have your way with me on a desktop."

"Don't be silly," Jenny said. "I agreed to marry you because I love you. But we really should do something to celebrate our engagement. And I say what better way and what better time, than right here and now?"

He cast a doubtful glance at the small desktop. "But how good can it be . . . ?"

"It's all in how good we make it." Jenny shot him a decidedly wicked smile that was all her own and reached for the buttons on his shirt. "And with what I have in mind, you'll be begging for more . . ."

Robert's eyes darkened. "Sweetheart, I guarantee that by the time we're done, I won't be the only one begging."

The way he was looking at her, with those sexy eyes all hot and focused, made her positively woozy. And while she wasn't the least bit psychic, she could definitely see some begging in her future.

"I hope you realize"—Jenny gazed up at him through lowered lashes—"this is only one of a whole list of fantasies that I'll be asking you to fulfill."

"And I hope *you* realize," Robert said, moving his hand to the small of her back and bringing her close against him, "that I'll always be up to the task."

If the hardness pressed against her was any indication, Jenny didn't have any doubts.

As his lips lowered to hers, she couldn't help but smile. Something told her that a lifetime wasn't going to be near long enough for them to explore all the bad-girl pleasures she had in mind.

AVON

978-0-06-124085-0
$13.95

978-0-06-112864-6
$13.95 ($17.50 Can.)

978-0-06-089023-0
$13.95 ($17.50 Can.)

978-0-06-078555-0
$13.95 ($17.50 Can.)

978-0-06-085199-6
$13.95 ($17.50 Can.)

978-0-06-081705-3
$13.95 ($17.50 Can.)

Visit www.AuthorTracker.com for exclusive
information on your favorite HarperCollins authors.

Available wherever books are sold, or call 1-800-331-3761 to order.

ATP 0707